She was the we
Twelve years ag
soon. Now the t
them.

Or at least for him. 'Forgive me,' Gustavo said gently. 'I just wish I could turn the clock back to before tonight, but I can't decide how far back to go.'

'To the last moment of happiness?' Joanna said. 'Or the last moment before a terrible mistake? Or perhaps it doesn't matter, and we'd make the same mistake again.'

'Joanna, you're talking mysteries. What mistake could you ever have made?'

She shook her head. 'I cannot tell you. You must let me have my secrets.'

But he too shook his head. 'No, I want to know your secrets. Every one of them. I want to know what you're thinking and feeling. I want—I want *you*."

Lucy Gordon cut her writing teeth on magazine journalism, interviewing many of the world's most interesting men, including Warren Beatty, Richard Chamberlain, Roger Moore, Sir Alec Guinness and Sir John Gielgud. She also camped out with lions in Africa, and had many other unusual experiences which have often provided the background for her books. She is married to a Venetian, whom she met while on holiday in Venice. They got engaged within two days. Two of her books have won the Romance Writers of America RITA award, SONG OF THE LORELEI and HIS BROTHER'S CHILD, in the Best Traditional Romance category. You can visit her website at www.lucy-gordon.com

Recent titles by the same author:

A FAMILY FOR KEEPS
THE MONTE CARLO PROPOSAL
GINO'S ARRANGED BRIDE

THE ITALIAN'S RIGHTFUL BRIDE

BY
LUCY GORDON

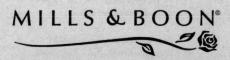

MILLS & BOON®

First published in Great Britain 2005
Harlequin Mills & Boon Limited,
Eton House, 18-24 Paradise Road, Richmond, Surrey TW9 1SR

© Lucy Gordon 2005

ISBN 0 263 84237 1

Set in Times Roman 10½ on 12 pt.
02-0605-45398

Printed and bound in Spain
by Litografia Rosés, S.A., Barcelona

PROLOGUE

'"*SOLID gold vases, mouth-watering jewels, wealth beyond the dreams of avarice.*"'

Joanna, stretched out on the beach, turned her head to where her ten-year-old son was sitting on the sand beside her, his head in a newspaper.

'What are you on about, darling?'

'Big find,' he said, peering at her over the top. 'Palace, fabulous treasure.' He saw her regarding him with amused disbelief and said, 'Well, they found a few old bricks, anyway.'

'That sounds more like it.' She laughed. 'I'm used to the way you embellish things. Where did they find these "old bricks"?'

'Rome,' he said, giving her the paper.

Following his pointing finger, she saw a small item with a few basic details.

'"*Fascinating and unique foundations—vast palace—fifteen hundred years old—*"'

'It sounds right up your street, Mum,' Billy observed. 'Ruins, crumbling with age—'

'If that's meant to be a comment on my appearance, you can save it,' she told him. 'I may look merely ancient but I feel prehistoric.'

'That's what I thought,' he said cheekily.

'I'll send you to bed without any supper.'

'You and what army?' he challenged her.

His face was wicked and gleeful. She adored him.

Because her job took her away from home, and she

was sharing Billy with her ex-husband, they saw too little of each other. This summer they were treating themselves to a holiday at Cervia, on the Adriatic coast of Italy.

It had been glorious to have nothing to do but stretch out on the beach and talk to Billy, who was mature for his years. But for both of them inactivity had soon begun to pall, and the newspaper item stirred all her professional instincts.

She had a glittering reputation as an archaeologist, or a 'rubble and bone merchant' as Billy irreverently put it, and this was, as he'd said, right up her street. As she read she hummed softly under her breath.

Foundations of huge building found in the grounds of the Palazzo Montegiano, ancestral home of the hereditary princes of Montegiano, and the residence of the present Prince Gustavo.

The humming stopped.

'Have you ever been to Rome, Mum?' Billy asked. 'Mum? *Mum?*'

Receiving no reply, he leaned closer and waved his hands. 'Earth to Mum. Come in, please.'

'Sorry,' she said hastily. 'What did you say?'

'Have you ever been to Rome?'

'Er—yes—yes—'

'You sound half-witted,' he said kindly.

'Do I, darling? Sorry, it's just—he always said there was a great lost palace.'

'He? You know this Prince Thingy?'

'I met him once, years ago,' she said vaguely. 'How about an ice cream?'

Steering him away from the subject was an act of desperation. Because there was no way she could say to her darling son, 'Gustavo Montegiano is the man I once loved more than I ever loved your father, the man I could have married if I'd been sufficiently selfish.'

And she might have added, 'He's the man who broke my heart without even knowing that he possessed it.'

CHAPTER ONE

'RING, damn you, ring!'

Prince Gustavo fixed his gaze on the phone, which stayed obstinately dead.

'You were supposed to call every week, without fail,' he growled. 'And it's been two weeks.'

Silence.

He got up from his desk and went impatiently over to the tall windows through which he could see the stone terrace. On the last of the broad steps that led down to the lawn sat a nine-year-old girl, her shoulders hunched in childish misery.

The sight increased Gustavo's anger. He strode back, snatched up the telephone and dialled with sharp, stabbing movements.

He knew nobody had ever forced his ex-wife to do what didn't suit her. But this time he was going to insist, not for himself, but for the little girl who pined for some sign that her mother remembered her.

'Crystal?' he snapped at last. 'You were supposed to call.'

'*Caro,*' came the soft purr that had once sent shivers up his spine. 'If you only knew how busy I am—'

'Too busy for your daughter?'

'My poor little Renata? How is she?'

'Pining for her mother,' he said furiously. 'And now I've got you on the line you're going to talk to her.'

'But, sweetie, I've no time. You caught me on my way out, and please don't call again—'

'Never mind going out,' he said. 'Renata's just outside and she can be here in a moment.' He could hear the little girl's footsteps running along the terrace.

'I have to go,' came Crystal's voice. 'Tell her I love her.'

'I'm damned if I will. Tell her yourself. Crystal— *Crystal?*'

But she had gone, hanging up at the exact moment the child came running into the room.

'Let me talk to Mamma,' she cried, seizing the phone from him. *'Mamma, Mamma.'*

He saw the joy drain out of her face as she heard the dead tone. And, as he'd feared, the face she then turned on him was full of accusation.

'Why didn't you let me talk to her?' she cried.

'Darling, she was in a rush—it was a bad time for her—'

'No, it was your fault. I heard you shouting at her. You don't want her to talk to me.'

'That isn't true—'

He tried to take his daughter into his arms but she resisted him, not by struggling but by standing stiff, her face blank and unrevealing.

Just like me, he thought sadly, remembering the times in his life when he had concealed his innermost self in the same way. There was no doubt that this was truly his child, unlike Crystal's second offspring, whose birth had precipitated the divorce.

'Darling…' he tried again, but gave up in the face of her silent hostility.

She blamed him for her mother's desertion and the fact that she'd been left behind, because she couldn't bear to believe anything else. And was it kinder to force the truth on her, or go along with her fantasy of a mother who yearned for her and a cruel father who kept them apart? He only wished he knew.

Reluctantly he released her and she ran out at once. Gustavo sat down heavily at his desk and buried his head in his hands.

'Have I come at a bad time?'

Gustavo looked up to see an elderly man in shabby, earth-stained clothes who stood in the tall window, mopping his brow.

'No, come in,' Gustavo said with relief, opening an ornate eighteenth-century cupboard and revealing a small fridge concealed inside.

'How is it going?' he asked, pouring two beers.

'I've gone about as far as I can,' Professor Carlo Francese said, puffing from his recent exertions. 'But my expertise is limited.'

'Not in my experience,' Gustavo said loyally.

They had been friends for eight years, ever since Gustavo had allowed his *palazzo* to be used for an archaeological convention. Carlo was an archaeologist with a major reputation, and when ancient foundations had recently been discovered on Gustavo's estate he had called Carlo first.

'Gustavo, this is potentially the biggest find for a century, and you need serious professionals. Fentoni is the best. He'll jump at it.'

He gave Gustavo a shrewd look. 'You're not listening.'

'Of course I am, it was just—*hell and damnation!*'

'Crystal?'

'Who else? It's not so much that she betrayed me with another man, bore him a son and made a fool of me. I hate that, but I can bear it. What I can't forgive is the way she left without a backward glance at Renata, and doesn't bother to keep in touch. My little girl is breaking her heart, and I can't help her.'

'I never much liked Crystal,' Carlo admitted slowly. 'I remember meeting her a few years after your wedding. You were totally crazy about her but she always struck me as slightly detached.'

'Totally crazy,' he murmured with a wry, reminiscent grin. 'That's true. I went on believing in her far too long, but I had to. In order to marry her I behaved very badly to someone else that I should have married, and I suppose I needed to believe that the ''prize'' I'd won was worth it.'

'Behaved badly?' The professor's eyes gleamed with interest. 'You mean really badly?'

'Sorry to disappoint you,' Gustavo said with a reluctant grin, 'but there was no grand drama. Neither the lady nor I were in love. It was to be a suitable marriage, virtually an arranged one.'

Carlo wasn't shocked. Whatever the modern world might imagine, such things were still common among the great aristocratic families of Europe. Money gravitated to titles, and where vast estates and ancient houses were concerned it was a matter of family duty to protect them.

And if there was one thing Gustavo understood it was his duty.

'So what happened about this arranged marriage?' Carlo asked now.

'My father was alive then, and he'd had some bad luck. A friend of my mother's knew of an English girl who had a great fortune. I met her, and we got on well.'

'What was she like?'

Gustavo considered for a moment.

'She was a nice person,' he said at last. 'Gentle and understanding, someone I could talk to. We would have had a good marriage, in a sedate kind of way. But then Crystal appeared, and suddenly sedate wasn't enough.

'She was—' he struggled for words '—like a comet flaming across the sky. She dazzled me. I couldn't see the truth, which was that she was ruthless and selfish. I saw it later, but by then we were married.'

'How did you break it off with your fiancée?'

'I didn't. She broke it off with me. She was wonderful. She'd seen what was happening and said that, if I preferred Crystal, there was no problem. After all, what woman wanted a reluctant husband? That was how she put it, and it all sounded so reasonable.'

'Suppose she'd refused to release you? Would you have gone through with the wedding?'

'Of course.' Gustavo sounded slightly shocked. 'I'd given my word of honour.'

'What about your family's reaction?'

'They weren't pleased but there was nothing they could do. We presented it to the world as a mutual decision, which in many ways it was, since I think my fiancée was secretly glad to be rid of me.'

He grinned.

'When I say "we" presented it to the world, I really mean that *she* did. She did all the talking while I stood there like a dummy and probably looking like one. My father was furious at losing her inheritance.'

'Crystal was poor, then?'

'No, she had a fortune, but it was more modest.'

'So you didn't put family interests first that time?' Carlo observed. 'Crystal must have been quite something.'

Gustavo nodded and fell silent, remembering the impact his wife had made on his younger self. She'd been all laughter and sensuality, reckless and passionately emotional, or so he'd thought. It was only later that he'd understood how limited was her capacity for any honest emotion.

He'd fallen into the trap of thinking that because her feelings were freely expressed, they must be deep. With himself it was the opposite. His feelings were too intense to be spoken of, and so the world mistakenly called him chilly.

But the friend watching him sympathetically at this moment knew better. He did not persist with the subject.

'The sooner you get this place studied by Fentoni and his team the better,' he observed.

'I suppose he's expensive,' Gustavo said wryly.

'The best always is. I guess money's tight again?'

'Crystal wants every last penny back. She's entitled to it, but it's a strain.'

'Well, perhaps this discovery will turn out to be a gold-mine.'

'To be sure,' Gustavo said without conviction. 'All right, let's contact him.'

Carlo snatched up the phone. 'I'll do it now.'

While he was getting through Gustavo returned to the window to look out over the lawns to where he could see his daughter in the distance. She was sitting on a tree stump, her knees drawn up, her arms clasped around them.

She looked up and, although she was too far off for him to discern her face, he was sure her expression was hostile. He smiled and waved to her, but she looked away.

He wanted to bang his head against the wall, riven with guilt and despair that he couldn't make things right for her.

Carlo was chattering urgently into the phone, sounding exasperated.

'Fentoni, old friend, this is a far more important job— Oh, damn your contract. Tell them you've changed your mind and want to do this instead— *How much?* Oh, I see.'

He looked up at Gustavo with a shrug of resignation.

'So who else, then?' he said back into the phone. 'Yes, I've heard of her, but if Mrs Manton is English, do we want her pronouncing on Italian artefacts? All right, I'll take your word for that. Have you got her number?'

He scribbled something down, and came off the phone to find Gustavo scowling.

'English?'

'Specialising in Italy,' Carlo told him. 'Fentoni says she was his best pupil. Why don't you let me deal with this? I'll contact her, fix a visit, you can see what you think of her, and then agree terms.'

'Thanks, Carlo. I'll leave everything in your hands.'

When Joanna Manton received the call on her cellphone, and understood what Carlo wanted, she had only one question.

'Are you saying that Prince Gustavo actually asked for me?'

'No, no,' his voice came down the line. 'You were recommended by Professor Fentoni. I suggest you come down and look the place over.'

She was silent, torn by temptation. Surely it could do no harm to see Gustavo again after twelve years? She was no longer a girl, buffeted by feelings she couldn't control.

It would even do her good to see him. Like her, he would be older, different, and the image that had persisted in her heart, defying all attempts to remove it, would be supplanted by reality. And at last she would be free.

'I was planning to spend the summer knocking about with my ten-year-old son,' she said.

'Bring him with you. His Excellency has a daughter of the same age. When shall I expect you?'

'I don't know…' she wavered.

Billy, who had been shamelessly eavesdropping her end of the conversation, mouthed, 'Montegiano?'

She nodded.

'Tell him you'll go.'

'Billy!'

'Mum, you want this job so much you can taste it. You know you do.' He grabbed the phone and spoke into it. 'She's on her way.' Catching her indignant look, he said innocently, 'I'm just trying to stop you wasting a lot of time. Why do women always dither?'

Secretly she was glad he'd taken the decision out of her hands. She told Carlo that she would be there in a few days, and hung up.

'Billy, I thought you wanted us to enjoy ourselves.'

He gave her a hilarious grin. 'But, Mum, we hate enjoying ourselves. It's so boring.'

She shared his laughter. He was a kindred spirit.

The next morning they piled everything into the car and set off to travel the five hundred miles across Italy, to the outskirts of Rome. As she neared their destination she found herself slowing down, making excuses for the delay.

'We'll stay here tonight,' she said when they reached the edge of the little town of Tivoli.

'But it's only another fifteen miles to Rome,' he protested.

'I'm tired,' she said quickly, 'and I'd rather arrive early tomorrow, after a good night's sleep.'

Later that night, when Billy had gone to bed, she sat by her window, looking in the direction that led to Rome, and called herself a coward.

Whyever had she agreed to do this? Some things were best left in the past. Yet the truth was that part of her was still the eighteen-year-old Lady Joanna who'd agreed to meet Prince Gustavo as a prospective husband, but in a mood of amused indulgence because Aunt Lilian, who'd planned everything, was such a dear.

'I'm not really interested,' she'd told her on the night before Gustavo arrived. 'Fancy linking us up because he needs my money and you want me to be a princess.'

Aunt Lilian had winced. 'That's a very vulgar way of putting it. In our world the right people must meet the right people.'

By 'our world' she'd meant wealth and titles. Joanna had an earl among her relatives and a huge fortune, so she was included in the charmed circle, which, even in a modern, supposedly democratic age, remained mostly closed to outsiders.

Joanna had thought all this was hilarious. How young she had been, how full of modern ideas! How sure that she knew it all! How stupidly, cruelly, fatally ignorant!

Sometimes fairy tales came true. Sometimes the sun shone, the birds sang and moon rhymed with June.

That summer had been a time of magic, when the Good Fairy had cast her spell, and everything was perfect for a brief moment.

Even twelve years later, just closing her eyes and letting her mind roam free could bring back the warmth and the sense of once-in-a-lifetime sweetness.

There had been a week-long house party, given by her second cousin, the earl, Lord Rannley, at his stately home in England, Rannley Towers.

She'd first seen Gustavo walking across the lawn towards the house. He was some way off so she had had several minutes to notice everything about him.

He was over six feet, with dark hair and a lean body, moving with a controlled grace that had held her entranced attention. It had been a hot day and he'd rolled up the sleeves of his shirt and pulled open the throat.

And that was how he lived in her mind ever after, Prince Charming in the story, handsome and elegant. Everything was perfect, too perfect to be true, if only she'd had the sense to see it.

But she'd lost all her common sense by the time he reached her, one of her cousins introduced them and he had said, in his quiet voice, '*Buon giorno, signorina.* It is a great pleasure to meet you.'

Nobody had warned her that it was possible for the world to turn upside down in a moment because of a young man with dark eyes and a gentle gravity that went straight to her heart.

But it had happened, and after that there was no turning back.

Naturally nobody mentioned the reason for the meeting. Officially Gustavo was travelling to see something of the world, and was calling on old friends of his father. But when the family sat down to dinner he was seated beside Joanna.

She had a hard time dressing for that meal. Now that she'd seen him she examined her own appearance critically.

'And I'm nothing much,' she sighed. 'I'm too tall, too thin—'

'Not thin,' Aunt Lilian protested loyally. 'Slender.'

'Thin,' she said stubbornly.

'Most girls would give their eye-teeth to be your size. If you took a little trouble you'd be beautiful and elegant.'

'Not beautiful. Not me.'

Aunt Lilian groaned, but there was some justice in Joanna's complaint. Her hair was fair, not blonde but mousy, her figure coltish rather than elegant. Her face was pleasant despite a slightly irregular mouth and a nose that she wished a fraction shorter. Her eyes were her best feature, being a restful grey, but it wasn't the deep blue she would have liked. Everything about her just missed being something better, and she had never been so acutely aware of it as now.

The dress she chose was a restrained blue silk which had cost the earth and did little for her. After trying her hair up, then down, then up, she finally let it hang loose about her shoulders. Her make-up was like the dress, restrained, chiefly because she lacked the self-confidence to be bold.

Nobody could have faulted Gustavo's behaviour over dinner. He talked to everyone and didn't try to monopolise Joanna. But when he turned to her she felt as though the rest of the room had vanished.

She didn't know what they talked about either then or over the next few days. They went riding together. There was laughter and idle chatter, and sometimes she would find him looking at her with a serious expression that made her heart turn over.

Halfway through the week he invited her out to a restaurant. He was the perfect host, charming, attentive, but not, to her disappointment, flirtatious. He asked about her life and she told him about how she'd lived since her parents died and her Aunt Lilian had raised her.

He told her about his own life on the Montegiano estate, and the love in his voice told her why he was prepared to put his home before everything else in his life.

'For six hundred years my family have lived in the same house,' he told her, 'always adding to it and making it more beautiful.'

'It sounds wonderful,' she told him eagerly. 'I love old places.'

'I would like you to see it.'

When they were drinking wine, he said with a touch of ruefulness, 'You know what our friends plan for us, don't you?'

Her heart began to beat faster. Was he going to propose right now?

But when she nodded he only said, 'We must not let them make complicated something that should be very simple. This is our decision, not theirs. There can be nothing without affection and respect.'

The words 'affection and respect' chilled her slightly, for they fell far short of what she wanted. But for a while it was enough to be here with him, intoxicated by his presence, falling more deeply in love with every passing second.

Afterwards they went to a nightclub, and danced together. At last, after so much dreaming and hoping, she was in the circle of his arms, feeling his hand firm on her waist, the warmth of his body moving against her. The sensation was so sweet as to be almost unbearable.

She was wildly, passionately in love. She knew now that the songs and the stories were right after all. The world was bathed in a golden light and soon heaven would be hers.

At the end of the week he invited her and Aunt Lilian to visit his estate just outside Rome. She was in seventh heaven. Of course he wanted to show her his home before making any final decisions.

She was so sure she understood him that even his reticence did not trouble her too much. He was naturally quiet and controlled. But that was only on the surface. Behind his barriers she sensed another man, vibrant, thrilling, waiting for the right woman to free his heart.

She knew she could be that woman, because they were alike. She too was quiet and retiring, and they would have a meeting of minds leading on inevitably to a meeting of hearts.

That, at any rate, was what she told herself.

The Montegiano estate only increased Joanna's sense of magic. Standing about three miles outside Rome, it covered a thousand acres, culminating in the great palace that stood on a rise, dominating the surrounding landscape.

For someone as much in love with the past as Joanna the house was a marvel. Down long corridors she wandered, meeting ancestors who looked down from centuries past. Gustavo described them in a way that brought them to life for her, and was clearly impressed by her knowledgeable interest.

'You know a great deal about history, and especially of my country,' he said, smiling.

'I've always been crazy about the past. I went on an archaeological dig once, and loved it. I'd probably go to college and study archaeology if I wasn't...'

Just in time she stopped herself from saying, If I wasn't going to get married, and hastily substituted, 'if I wasn't the sort of person who dithers about deciding things.'

She knew she was being studied by every employee in

the place, all waiting with bated breath for the announcement.

Day after day she and Gustavo rode together, and he told her about the estate he loved in a voice that was gentle, almost emotional. One day as they walked through the woods he said, 'Do you like my home, Joanna?'

'I love it,' she said fervently.

'Do you think you could be happy living here?'

That was his proposal.

She accepted so quickly that the memory made her blush later. She brushed her fears aside, desperate to seize her heart's desire.

When, at last, he kissed her it made her forget everything else. There was skill in everything he did, covering her mouth, teasing her with his lips, caressing, holding her close. The effect on her was electric. Yet even then she was cautious enough to hold back a little, waiting until she could sense that his passion was as deep as her own.

The wedding was set to take place two months later, in England. Two weeks before the date Gustavo and his family arrived to stay at Rannley Towers and take part in a series of glittering festivities. In the weeks apart they corresponded, but mostly about practical affairs. They talked about the estate, the life they would live there. He addressed her as 'My dearest Joanna' and signed himself 'Yours affectionately'.

But when she saw him again nothing mattered but that he was here, and they would soon be married.

Her dress was a masterpiece of ivory silk, cut simply to suit her tall figure. The sleeves were long, almost down to the hem, the train stretched behind her and the veil streamed down to the floor and over the train. When she put it on and regarded herself in the mirror she knew that she was beautiful. Now, surely, he would fall in love with her?

And then Crystal arrived.

CHAPTER TWO

AT THE time she seemed like the wicked witch, but Joanna supposed that the bad fairy was more accurate, because Crystal actually looked like a fairy, being petite with blonde hair that fluffed about her face like candy-floss.

She had deep blue eyes, full of fun, a dainty nose, a mouth that was pure Cupid, and her delicious, gurgling laugh was irresistible. She was lovely, glamorous, enchanting.

Everything I wasn't.

Crystal had been invited to stay in the house by Frank, one of Joanna's many cousins, who was courting her. At their first meeting Joanna had liked her. Crystal charmed everyone with her beauty and her wicked sense of humour.

She had a way of talking rapidly, so that Gustavo often asked her to slow down or explain some English word to him. Several times Joanna heard her saying, 'No, no, you say it like this.'

Then she would dissolve into laughter at his pronunciation, and he would laugh with her.

Was it then that Joanna first sensed danger?

How can I tell? Whatever I sensed, I wouldn't admit it.

So many things: the burning look that flashed briefly in his eyes for Crystal, which had never been there for her. The way he watched the door until she entered, and relaxed when she appeared.

A hundred tiny little details, which she pretended meant nothing, until the day when it was no longer possible to pretend.

At first she thought he was alone. Coming from the brilliant sunlight into the trees, she saw only him, and her heart leapt before she noticed that he was leaning over and down towards the woman in his arms.

But then she saw them, and the way he was raining kisses on her upturned face, kissing her to the point of madness, again and again, so that Joanna knew that kisses would never be enough for him.

Kissing as he had never kissed her.

She stood and watched, her heart breaking, her world shattering around her.

She drew back behind a great oak, although it was needless. They were beyond noticing her or anything else. She heard him say,

'I'm sorry, my darling. I had no right to do this when I have nothing to offer you.'

'Why can't we be happy?' That was Crystal's voice. 'Don't you love me?'

'You know I love you,' he said, almost violently. 'I didn't know I could feel like this. If I had—'

He stopped. Joanna listened, her heart beating madly. If he had…

'If you'd met me first, you wouldn't have proposed to Joanna, would you?'

'Never,' he said hoarsely.

'Don't you want to marry me, my darling?'

'Don't ask me that.'

'But I must ask it,' she persisted in her soft, enticing voice. 'If we're going to lose each other, at least give me honesty.'

'All right, I want to marry you,' he said in a fierce,

passionate voice. 'I can't, but neither can I stop loving and wanting you. You're there with me every moment, night and day, waking or sleeping.'

'Then how can you cast me aside?'

'Because I have made promises to Joanna. My darling, I beg you to understand, I *must* keep those promises.'

'Why? She doesn't love you any more than you love her.'

'But we're a few days from our wedding. How can I humiliate her in front of the world?'

'Gustavo, have you thought of the future? All those years tied to a woman you don't love. How will you endure them?'

The silence that followed froze Joanna to the soul. Just a few seconds, but enough to make her feel that she was dying. At last his answer came in a voice that was bleak with despair.

'I'll survive, somehow.'

She'd thought her heart couldn't break any more, but when she heard that she knew she was wrong.

And strangely, it was the knowledge that there was nothing more to hope for that made it possible for her to step out from behind the tree, smiling and saying brightly, 'Isn't there something you want to tell me?'

Their faces were imprinted on her memory forever, Gustavo's pale and shocked, Crystal's with an expression she couldn't read. Only later did she think of cats and cream. At the time she was concentrating on what she must do.

Crystal spoke first, sounding suitably uneasy.

'Joanna, we didn't mean you to find out like this.'

'It doesn't matter how I found out,' she answered with a fair assumption of gaiety. 'The point is that we're still in time to put matters right.'

'I have no intention of asking you to free me.' Gustavo's voice was hollow.

'But perhaps I'd like to chuck you out,' she replied with a shrug. 'Oh, come on, this isn't the nineteenth century. The sky isn't going to fall if there's a last-minute change of plan.'

She never forgot the look on his face then, sheer blinding hope at the thought of not having to marry her.

'You—mean that?' he asked as though unable to believe his ears.

'Of course I mean it. Honestly, darling,' she added, using the term of endearment for the first time, 'if you're in love with someone else—well, why should I want you?'

'But the formalities—'

'Blow the formalities. We've changed our minds. Both of us. Come on, let's get it over with.'

She turned away quickly, not sure how long she could keep up the façade. As she began to walk she heard Gustavo call, 'Joanna…'

And there it was, the note she had dreamed of hearing in his voice, warm and emotional now that he was grateful for his release. She fled back to the house.

She had only the dimmest recollection of what followed. There was family uproar, scene after scene in which she did most of the talking, laughing as she insisted that it was a mutual decision and she couldn't be happier.

She doubted if anyone was fooled, especially as the engagement to Crystal came immediately after. But in the face of her determination there was nothing anybody could do.

A special licence was obtained with Crystal's name on it and the wedding was to go ahead on the same day in the same church, with one bride substituted for another. Joanna sailed through the whole process, apparently with not a care in the world. She dreaded their wedding, but knew she had to be there or the world would know why.

For a while the need to put on an act kept her mind on the terrible ache inside. At night she sobbed herself to sleep. By day she smiled and smiled and smiled.

By the night before the wedding the strain of weeping in secret was tearing her apart. She wanted to scream aloud, impossible in that house.

Outside it had begun to rain, water coming down in noisy torrents with the occasional thunderclap. Too distraught to think clearly, she threw on some clothes and left the house by a side-door, running across the grass towards the trees.

Deep in the wood she gave vent to her grief, crying like a wounded animal, and even once banging her head against a tree, screaming, 'Why—why—why?'

Why? Because he loves her and not you. Because she's beautiful and dazzling and you're dull and ordinary. Because all the money in the world isn't enough to make him want you.

When it was over she felt no better, just completely exhausted. She sank to the ground, leaning back against a tree trunk, whispering hoarsely, 'Why did I do it? Why did I give him up so easily? When we were married I could have made him love me.'

The regret made her start to weep again, but this time weakly, in helpless, devastating misery.

After an hour she dragged herself to her feet and stumbled out of the wood, desperate to get back to the house before the sun came up, and she could be seen.

She managed it, thankful that nobody had seen her, and ran up the back stairs until she reached the floor where her room was. She was almost there—the next corridor—

'Joanna!'

Her worst nightmare came true. Gustavo stood there in his dressing gown, astonished at the sight of her.

'Whatever has happened to you?' he said, concerned. 'You've been out in that rain?'

'It wasn't raining when I went out,' she said, struggling for words.

'But it's been raining for an hour.'

'I walked a long way. I needed some air. It took time to get back.' She had no idea what she was saying.

'You're hurt,' he said, looking at her forehead.

'I fell,' she gasped. 'I hit my head on a log.'

'You need a doctor. Let me—'

'Keep away from me.'

He was reaching gentle fingers towards her bruise, but she knew if he touched her she'd start screaming again.

'Your teeth are chattering,' he said, his hand falling. 'Go and have a hot bath or you'll catch cold. My dear, you've got water dripping from your hair and over your face.'

The water on her face wasn't rain. He stood there looking at her tears and didn't know it.

'Please look after yourself,' he said. 'I don't want you being too unwell for my wedding tomorrow, not when I owe it all to you.'

The warmth in his voice was her undoing. She fled to her own room and locked the door. Tearing off her clothes, she got under a hot shower and stayed there, not moving, just leaning against the tiled wall.

After a long time her brain started working again, enough to make her wonder how he'd come to be in that corridor at that hour. Then she remembered that it was near to where Crystal slept.

She'd thought her tears were all cried out, but she found she was wrong. This time it was the shower that disguised them.

Next day she sat in the body of the church, looking at Gustavo's back as he waited for his bride, then saw him turn and watch her approach with an expression of such total adoration that she closed her eyes. For a dreadful moment she actually feared she was going to faint, but she recovered and sat rigid as Crystal became his wife.

Now he was lost to her forever.

But he'd been lost anyway. Her regret of last night had been foolish. He might have married her, but he would never, ever have loved her.

The reception was followed by a ball at which she danced until she was ready to drop. That was how she met Freddy Manton, who seemed to appear from no-where, a friend of a friend of a friend. He was handsome, charming and a great dancer. Their steps blended perfectly, and they put on a bravura display that made the others applaud.

When the music became soft and tender Joanna and Freddy danced again, holding each other romantically close. It was her way of telling the world that she didn't care whom Gustavo married. She hoped he would notice.

But when he waltzed past with Crystal clasped in his arms, Joanna knew that he was oblivious to everyone else in the world. His bride's face was raised to his, and for a cruel moment Joanna saw the worship in his gaze. She closed her eyes, feeling her brave pretence shatter around her.

At last it was time for the bride and groom to leave for their honeymoon. Joanna had wanted to go straight to Italy, but Crystal had set her heart on Las Vegas, and Gustavo could refuse her nothing.

Determined to play out the charade to the end, Joanna joined the crowd waving them off. Was it accident or spite that made Crystal toss the bouquet to her? She caught it instinctively, before she could stop herself, then stood there, clutching the bouquet that should always have been hers.

It was only later that she fully understood what that day had done to her. She had passed through the fire and emerged stronger, because something that had been burned to ash could never be burned again.

She enrolled in college, studied archaeology and blanked out grief by working herself into the ground.

'If you ask me you had a nervous breakdown,' Aunt Lilian said later. 'Whenever I saw you, you looked as if you were dying. And instead of being sensible like other girls, and taking a cruise, you made everything worse by working away at those awful books.'

But far from making things worse, Joanna knew that 'those awful books' had saved her. After a year her tutors were predicting great things for her.

Grief finally subsided into a dull ache that she managed to push aside in the fascination with the subject she loved.

She made herself a promise. Never again would she allow herself to feel anything with the depth and intensity she'd felt for Gustavo. She knew she couldn't stand it a second time.

She was safe now. She could protect herself from hurt. But she had paid a terrible price.

She began going to parties again, even enjoying them. Finally, one evening, as she was sipping champagne—

'Fancy meeting you here!'

It was Freddy Manton, beaming at her.

'I looked for you later but you'd vanished,' he said. 'I've been heartbroken ever since.'

'You don't look very heartbroken.' She laughed.

They began seeing each other. He was good company, merry, slightly feckless, but kind-hearted. She was lonely, and managed to persuade herself that her affection for him would be enough. They married while she was still at college and she became pregnant immediately, only just managing to get her exams out of the way before rushing to the hospital for Billy's arrival.

To do Freddy justice, he really tried, managing to be faithful for a whole four years, a record for him. For Billy's sake they stayed together for another four years, until his infidelities exasperated her beyond bearing.

The divorce was amicable. If she'd been really in love with him their parting would have hurt more than it did.

She knew almost nothing about Gustavo in the intervening years. Recently she had chanced to pick up a newspaper bearing the announcement that Their Excellencies Prince and Princess Montegiano had been blessed with a son and heir, their first child since the birth of their daughter ten years previously.

So the marriage had flourished, she thought. She had done the right thing.

It worked out well for both of us, she mused now. Life's gone well for me too. I'm in control, settled, even happy. My job is great, I'm friendly with my ex. I have a son I adore and who thinks I'm 'OK'—a big compliment from a ten-year-old boy. I'm one of the lucky ones.

So why did I return here?

She looked out at the quiet streets of Tivoli, then past them to the vista that led to Rome.

Because after all these years, it's time to exorcise the ghost and be free to get on with my life.

She reached the gates of the Montegiano estate to find them exactly as she had last seen them. The gatekeeper called to the house and received a message to let her in. Driving the long road to the house was like a rewind of her previous experience.

She chatted calmly to Billy, refusing to think of what would happen in a few minutes when she would see him for the first time in twelve years.

Crystal would be there and she would see them together, husband and wife. The sight of their domesticity would be the final piece in the puzzle.

At last the huge *palazzo* came in sight, just as she remembered it, broad white marble steps sweeping up between tall, elegant columns. As her car neared an elderly man came out and stood waiting, a smile of welcome on his face.

'I'm Professor Carlo Francese,' he said, shaking her hand. 'We spoke on the phone. I'll be your host while Gustavo's away.'

He wasn't here. Her heart skipped a beat.

But it was good, she told herself. She needed no distractions.

Billy and Carlo took to each other at once, she was glad to see.

'You're in the Julius Caesar room,' Carlo explained. 'It's always given to the guest of honour.'

She almost said, Yes, I know. The room had been hers when she was last here.

It had changed a lot, and she could see that money had been spent reviving it. It now looked new, shining, and, to Joanna's eye, less charming. Billy had been given the room next door, which was equally grandiose and reduced him to fits of laughter.

After a wash and brush-up she knocked on his door. He joined her, looking around him at the gorgeous hallway, with its marble columns and frescoed ceiling.

'What a place!' he said with an appreciative whistle.

'It is, isn't it?' she agreed. 'What's up, Billy?' He had turned suddenly.

'I just thought I saw someone on the stairs. There.'

They looked just in time to see the pale face of a little girl staring up at them with hostility. Then she vanished.

Joanna went downstairs, braced to see Crystal, but there was no sign of her. Carlo ushered them into a magnificent room with tall windows overlooking the lawns, and immediately plunged into talking about the foundations that had been discovered.

Billy listened, asking some intelligent questions, to Joanna's pride. But then something seemed to distract him, and he slipped away.

'We saw a little girl upstairs,' Joanna ventured.

'That would be Renata,' Carlo said at once. 'Gustavo's daughter.' He sighed. 'Poor child.'

'Why poor? Is she jealous now that she has a little brother?'

Carlo looked around and dropped his voice.

'Gustavo's divorce has just become final. The little boy wasn't his, and his wife has taken the child to live with her lover.'

Joanna drew in a sharp breath.

'His—you mean Crystal?'

'Yes; do you know her?'

'We met briefly many years ago, but I haven't stayed in touch. I didn't know this.'

'As you can imagine, it's hit Gustavo very hard, so we

don't talk about it. But I thought you should know the situation.'

'Yes,' she said slowly. 'Yes, I'm glad you warned me.'

Carlo didn't seem to notice anything odd in her manner.

'When you're ready we'll go and see the dig,' he said. 'It's about a mile away.'

'I can't wait.'

As soon as she saw the discovery Joanna knew she had come to the right place. Her personal feelings didn't matter. This was the find of the century, and it *had* to be hers.

From the corner of her eye she could see Renata and Billy. They seemed to have established perfect rapport, and she was showing him around the site, pointing out places of interest. After a while they strolled away together.

She spent the rest of the day with Carlo, becoming more convinced that this really was the great lost palace Gustavo had spoken of. At dinner that evening she met Laura, a smiling, middle-aged woman who looked after Renata. To Joanna's amusement Billy turned his charm on her and within minutes Laura was lost.

'You and Renata seem to get on well,' she said to him as they climbed the stairs later that night.

'She's been telling me about Prince Gustavo,' Billy said, frowning. 'Honestly, Mum, he's a monster. You know her mother's gone?'

'Yes, Carlo told me.'

'Apparently he drove her out and wouldn't let Renata go with her. He actually grabbed hold of Renata and kept her here by force. She says he's full of hate and he's taking it out on her.'

'Billy, I don't believe that,' she said at once.

'Why?' he asked.

'Well—'

'Why not, Mum? You always said, "Stick to the evidence." Where's the evidence that Renata's wrong?'

She was caught, since she could hardly say that she'd known Gustavo and this wasn't like him. And how well had she known him?

'Sometimes I wish I hadn't brought you up to be so logical,' she sighed.

'Too late now.'

'Let's wait and hear the evidence for the other side,' she countered.

'That's right, Mum. When he gets here you ask him what really happened.'

'Go to bed,' she said firmly. 'And stop being cheeky.'

He gave his wicked grin. 'It's too late for that too,' he said, and vanished into his room before she could think of an answer.

Within two days Joanna had assembled a crack team, all of them people who had worked with her on other digs. Plunging into work was a relief. It took her mind off Gustavo and the situation she'd found.

She resisted the picture Billy had drawn, of a man so enraged that he cruelly penalised his child. But she, more than anyone, knew how he'd adored Crystal, and how her desertion must have devastated him. What had bitterness and misery done to him?

She could hardly believe that Renata was Gustavo and Crystal's child since she looked like neither of them. Her little face lacked any hint of her mother's beauty, being round and plump. Joanna, who remembered her own childhood, when she'd felt plain and dull, sympathised with her.

But Renata's eyes were intelligent. She would sit with

Billy and his mother, sharing their snack, but saying nothing until suddenly, like the bursting of a dam, she would make an awkward attempt to reach out.

'Billy told me about his father,' she blurted out once. 'He says you're divorced.'

'Yes, we are,' Joanna said gently.

'My parents are divorced.'

'I've heard.'

'Billy says his father's always calling him on his cell-phone.'

'That's right. Several times a week.'

'My mother calls me every single day,' Renata said defiantly. 'She bought me a cellphone just for the two of us, because she says she couldn't get through the day without talking to me.'

'That's a lovely thing for her to say.'

'Sometimes she cries because Papa won't let us be together. But Mamma says one day she's going to come and rescue me, and then we're going to run away to the end of the world, where Papa can't find us.'

Her voice had been growing more wobbly as she spoke, until she was forced to stop. Joanna saw her turn away to wipe her eyes, and wondered if she was weeping because of her father's unkindness or because she knew it was all a fantasy. She felt helpless.

Billy had listened to this, saying nothing, but watching Renata with kindly eyes. At last he drew her away, giving his mother a brief nod, as if to say that he would take over now.

He's years older than ten, she thought with a wry smile.

As the days wore on the heat mounted until the after-noons were almost unbearable.

'All right, guys, time for a break,' she called out one

day when it was nearly one o'clock. 'Take a siesta; come back when it's cooler.'

They headed for the house, eager to find shade. As often before, Joanna didn't go with them. She loved being left alone with the work, not doing anything, simply absorbing the past.

She brushed earth from her clothes, thankful that she'd worn wide canvas trousers that let in some air to cool her legs. Over them she had a man's shirt, tied at the waist with one of Freddy's old ties that she kept for the purpose. Her head was protected by a vast-brimmed canvas hat.

She loved to stretch out in the warmth, even though someone as fair-skinned as herself had to work hard not to be burned. Years of working in the sun had turned her a permanent light brown, and bleached her hair.

She kicked off her old canvas shoes and lay flat on the ground, arms flung wide, head obliterated by the huge hat. She supposed she looked like a hobo, but she didn't care. This was bliss.

Beginning to doze, she was only vaguely aware of a car stopping nearby. She sensed rather than heard someone looming over her then dropping to one knee.

'Go away,' she muttered. 'I'm asleep.'

'Excuse me…'

The man's voice was polite but firm, and there was power in the hand that grasped her shoulder. Reluctantly Joanna moved the hat aside and looked up.

At first she couldn't see properly. His head blotted out the sun, throwing his face into darkness.

'Who are you?' she asked, grumpy at being disturbed.

But she knew before he replied. Her vision was clearing and the face gazing quizzically down at her was the one she would never forget.

CHAPTER THREE

SHE sat up, studying him. He was older, heavier, with a careworn look that did not belong on a man of only thirty-four. She saw that much in an instant, also the touch of premature grey at the sides of his head.

He was frowning at her. 'Have we met before?'

'We did once,' she told him gently. 'A long time ago.'

'Forgive me…' He searched her face. 'It will come to me in a moment.'

'Time changes us all,' she said with a wry smile. 'I might not have recognised you if I hadn't been prepared. And twelve years is a long time.'

'Twelve—? *Maria Vergine! Joanna!*'

'At last!' she chuckled, having regained her composure enough to see the funny side. 'How unflattering you are!'

He reddened, and she remembered how shy he could sometimes be. It was odd, and appealing, in a man who lived at the peak of society.

'I didn't mean—well, as you say, old times. It's good to see you again. But how do you come to be here? Are you with…?' He indicated the dig.

'Yes, I did finally become an archaeologist.'

He reached out his hand to help her to her feet. It was as she remembered, lean but steely strong.

'It was always what you really wanted, I recall,' he said. 'You used to talk of it.'

'You mean I bent your ear endlessly,' she reminded him, dusting herself down. 'Goodness knows how you endured me!'

'I liked it. You were so passionate about your favourite subject, it made your eyes light up. So you finally achieved your ambition, and now work with Mrs Manton, who, Carlo assures me, is the very best. Why are you laughing?'

'I must thank Carlo for his good opinion.'

'His—? You mean—?'

Her eyes teased him. 'Uhuh!'

'*You* are Mrs Manton?'

'I plead guilty.'

He groaned. 'I don't know why it didn't occur to me, except that you're young to have such a reputation.'

'Ah, but I'm the best,' she reminded him, laughing.

'I'm sure you are. Well, it's good to know that an old friend is doing this work.'

'Not just me. I have a team that I use for big jobs. They've gone back to the house for some lunch.'

'Then let us do the same. It's too hot to stand out here.'

'Now I remember,' he said as they drove back. 'When Carlo called me he mentioned a team, and that you're all staying in the house.'

'I hope you don't mind your house being invaded. It keeps us close to the work.'

'Of course. Where else would you stay?'

Joanna was getting her bearings. She had seen him and, although an intensely attractive man, he was no longer the romantic Prince Charming of her memories. She was full of relief. Everything was going to be all right.

'I'll have our lunch served in my office and we can catch up on old times,' Gustavo said as they approached the house.

But in the same moment Carlo appeared at the top of the steps, waving gleefully as he saw them.

'It will have to wait,' Gustavo said. 'Let's go in so that I can meet your team.'

The next hour was taken up with introductions. Gustavo greeted everyone involved in the dig and joined them in the buffet lunch. He behaved perfectly, spending time with each one and giving them his whole attention.

Joanna knew that this was part of *noblesse oblige*, something he'd been taught from childhood as the gracious behaviour expected of a prince. But the effect was still charming, and she was amused to notice that the three young women in her team flowered under it.

Claire had only just left college, cheerfully called herself the dogsbody of the group, and obviously regarded Gustavo with almost schoolgirl admiration.

Raven-haired Lily was an anthropologist, a blazing beauty and an incurable romantic who fell in love in ten minutes and out again in five. One look was enough to tell Joanna that Lily was already far gone.

Even Sally, a short, stern young woman, who was always gruff except when dealing with computers, gazed up at Gustavo, her attention riveted.

It forced Joanna to see him through their eyes, not overlaid by memories of how he had been, but as the mature man he was now, and she had to admit that she understood their reaction.

He'd been very young when she had loved him, little more than a boy. Now the years had brought him to his prime, and his prime was splendid. He seemed to have actually grown, but had merely filled out. As a boy he'd been too lean for his height. Now the slight extra weight he carried made him impressive.

He smiled suddenly, and at last she saw something familiar. It was more of a half-smile, as though some part of him was holding back, concealed behind it. Just as it had always been.

'Does anyone know where my daughter is?' he asked, looking around.

'She's probably with my son,' Joanna told him. 'They get on well.'

'You have a son?' he said swiftly. 'How old?'

'Ten.'

'And your husband—is he with you here?'

'No, we divorced a couple of years back.'

'We must talk later. I want to hear all about you.'

'And I about you.' Then something caught her eye and she pointed to the door. 'That's Billy, coming in now, with Renata.'

He turned at once, smiling at the little girl, making a quick move towards her. For a very brief moment Renata smiled, but it was gone so quickly that it was clear she had suppressed it. When Gustavo tried to hug her she gave him only the slightest response.

'This is my son, Billy,' Joanna said, quickly moving over to them. 'Billy, this is Prince Gustavo.'

'Just Gustavo,' he said at once, extending his hand.

Billy shook it politely but Joanna was dismayed to notice that his manner was restrained, with none of his usual eager friendliness. Gustavo didn't react, but she had the feeling he'd noticed.

Hal, Joanna's right-hand man, was pouring himself a large beer, saying, 'OK, boss, what's the programme for this afternoon. Boss? *Boss?*'

She came back to the present.

'Sorry, were you talking to me?'

'Do I call anyone else boss?' he asked patiently.

'Not if you're wise. OK, this afternoon we're going to—'

'May I interrupt a moment?' Gustavo said smoothly. 'I just want to say that I hope you'll all join me for dinner tonight.'

'Do we have to dress posh?' Hal asked, looking at his magnificent surroundings. 'Because I forgot to bring my white tie and tails.'

'Informal dress, I promise,' Gustavo assured him. 'Now, if you'll excuse me, I must go.'

He touched Renata lightly on the shoulder, indicating with his head for her to follow him. But the child scowled and turned away. He watched her for a moment, and it seemed to Joanna that he was longing for her to turn back and smile at him. When she didn't, he walked out.

That evening Joanna soaked herself in water, allowing the tensions as well as the dust of the day to leave her.

She'd seen him and it had been a shock, because no matter how well prepared she'd thought herself, the reality had been nothing like her expectations. After twelve years, she thought, how else could it be? And how much had she changed in that time?

And whatever else was different, he was still as wickedly attractive as before. Watching the three other women had told her that.

She dressed herself in a pair of black velvet trousers and a brilliant-red silk blouse. In her ears she wore solid gold earrings.

She was dissatisfied with her hair, which she'd meant to trim back to shoulder-length, then forgotten. She had to settle for brushing it vigorously and hoping it wouldn't look too tousled.

Lily and Claire, who were sharing a room, joined her

in the corridor. Lily especially was looking forward to the coming evening, as her low-cut dress proclaimed.

'Just get him!' she exclaimed. '*Wow!* Is he fit or what?'

Joanna pretended to be shocked.

'Are you talking about His Excellency, Prince Gustavo Montegiano?' she asked. 'Come, come! Where's your respect for rank?'

'He can pull rank on me any time he likes,' Lily said, contriving to give the words a lascivious meaning. 'Come on, now, you've got to admit he's *wow*! Those eyes. Those muscles.'

'Don't you ever think about anything but men?' Sally asked, appearing with Hal, and falling into step beside them as they descended the stairs.

'Yes, but I spend too much time with the ones who've been dead for centuries,' Lily pointed out. 'Living fellers tend to look very good after that.'

'*I'm* living,' Hal said. Where Lily was concerned he existed in a permanent state of hope.

'Down, Fido!' Lily said.

'What happened to his wife?' Sally asked.

'They're divorced,' Joanna explained, keeping her voice low. 'But please don't talk about that.'

'Discretion is my middle name,' Lily said untruthfully. 'But honestly, was she crazy? Can you imagine any woman having *that*, and not clinging on for dear life?'

'Can we talk about something else?' Joanna asked tensely.

'Perhaps he's not as gorgeous as he looks,' Claire put in.

'And perhaps pigs fly,' Lily scoffed.

'No, I mean as a person,' Claire said. 'He might have a nasty temper—'

'He'd still be as sexy as hell!' Lily pointed out.

'Will you two hush?' Joanna said frantically. 'Not another word, in my hearing or out of it. Honestly, I can't take you anywhere.'

She remembered the dining room well. In this grandiose room she and Gustavo had been toasted on the night of their engagement. Now it had a livelier air.

It was a good evening with plenty of laughter. Carlo was there, also the children, with Laura. They had spent the last couple of hours riding. Renata was already skilled and Billy was learning.

'So that's where you were,' Gustavo said to Renata. 'I looked for you.'

Joanna watched the little girl, remembering the harsh things that, according to Billy, she had said about her father. Surely they could not be true?

Renata maintained a cool demeanour towards Gustavo, but when he wasn't looking at her she would fix her eyes on him with something that might have been longing. If he glanced back at her, she hurriedly turned away.

Gustavo wanted to hear all about the dig.

'I suppose it's too soon to have discovered anything significant,' he said.

'Much too soon,' Joanna said. 'We're still in what Hal calls the ''getting-dirty-with-nothing-to-show-for-it'' stage.'

In this way she tossed the ball to Hal, who, being naturally talkative, seized it. He then monopolised the conversation, although once he did say, 'You should really talk to the chief. She's a terrible slave-driver. We're all scared of her.'

Everyone laughed and Joanna said, 'So I should hope.'

She stayed mostly quiet, letting the others talk. Sometimes Gustavo darted a curious glance at her, but he seldom spoke to her, although she was sitting at right angles to him, at the head of the table.

After the meal Laura announced that it was time for the children to go to bed. Billy and Renata said their goodbyes politely. Renata allowed her father to kiss her cheek but she didn't kiss him back. Nor did he try to make her. He simply stood still while she left the room without a backward glance at him.

The sight of this big, impressive man seemingly beaten into submission by a child's hostility made something catch at Joanna's throat. She turned away, feeling as though she was invading his privacy.

Suddenly the evening had lost its savour for her, and, as though she had X-ray vision, she divined that it was the same with him. He talked and smiled, but a snub from a little girl had quenched a light inside him.

He did his duty to the last minute, escorting them up the stairs and saying goodnight as though he had all the time in the world. But she knew that secretly he was longing to escape, and her heart ached for him when first one person, then another had 'just one more thing' to say.

But at last it was all over, everyone had gone to their rooms and the corridor was quiet. Joanna noticed a faint beam of light coming from under Billy's door, and went in.

'You should be asleep, not reading,' she said.

'Honestly, Mum, how can anyone sleep with that racket going on outside?' he said, sounding aggrieved. 'Why do people always say goodnight at the tops of their voices?'

'All right,' she said, recognising some justice in this, without actually being fooled by it. 'They've all gone now, so put the book away.'

'OK, Mum.'

They hugged each other and she slipped out into the long, wide corridor. The lights had been turned low and it was a moment before she realised that she wasn't alone. Gustavo stood a few yards away, his hand resting on the handle of Renata's door.

It was on the far side, and a slight bend in the corridor meant that she could plainly make him out, even in the gloom. She saw him try the handle, then again, until he was forced to accept that the door was locked.

For a long moment he stood there. Then he spoke and Joanna thought he said, 'Please, my darling.'

When there was no reply he leaned his head against the door.

Joanna moved away very quietly, knowing that he must never realise that she had glimpsed his private pain. She managed to get into her room and close the door unseen, and stood leaning back against it, eyes closed.

She had come here hoping to find a scene of domestic contentment that would help her draw a line under the past. Instead she'd discovered misery, bitterness and the destruction of the very marriage she had sacrificed herself to bring about.

It was late and she supposed she ought to go to bed, but her mind was seething and she knew there would be no sleep tonight. All evening she'd been aware of Gustavo. While she sat near to him at the table she had sensed him through every fibre of her being, every breath she drew.

Now she was even more aware that his room was just opposite her own. She listened for the sound of his footsteps returning along the corridor, but then stopped, impatient with herself.

I ought to go away from here, she thought. Go! Go now!

But she knew she wasn't going to go.

She went to the window and looked out over the countryside, the fountain in the garden, lawns fading into the darkness of the trees. An owl hooted softly in the distance.

From here she could see exactly the place where she had stood one evening, longing for Gustavo to come out and share the moonlight with her. In the end he had joined her, but their conversation had been stilted and uneasy.

Suddenly the beauty of the night was irresistible. It called to her, promising at least a kind of peace after the tensions of the day. She hurried out into the corridor, down the stairs and out onto the stone terrace.

Does nothing about this place ever change? she thought. Then, now—it might be the same night.

But one thing was different, she realised as a sound from the corner made her turn her head in time to see the shadow sitting there unfold, stand and approach her.

'*Ciao,*' he said softly.

'How did you—?'

'How did I get here so quickly? I came down the back stairs. It was you in the corridor, wasn't it?'

'Yes, I'm sorry. I wasn't prying. I'd just been in to say goodnight to Billy and—'

'It's all right. You need not explain. I hoped that since I'd been away she might—well…' He shrugged.

Now she could see better in the darkness and she realised there was a low table with a bottle of wine and two fluted glasses. He filled one and handed it to her.

'Were you expecting someone?' she asked.

'Yes. You.'

She didn't waste time with arch questions. Of course he had known she would be here.

'It was so hot inside that I had to come out for some fresh air.'

Gustavo nodded. 'I come out here every night to sit quietly and let the cares and strains of the day fall away. They're always there again tomorrow, but this gets them into perspective.'

'Renata blames you for everything, doesn't she?'

'Is that a guess or do you have inside information?'

'Well, she talks to Billy a lot—'

'I thought that might be it, from the wary way he looked at me.'

'I'm sorry, he doesn't mean to be rude—'

'Don't be sorry. If she's got a friend she can talk to that's the best thing that could happen. I know she doesn't talk to anyone else, even Laura. And she needs someone because her life has been turned upside down in so many ways. I expect you know all about it by now.'

'I'd heard that you and Crystal weren't together any more.'

'Did you also hear that she bore a son by another man?'

'Yes,' she admitted.

'Well, then, you know everything,' he said heavily.

'Gustavo, I wish I knew what to say. It must have been terrible for you—'

But he shook his head. 'I don't matter. Renata loved her little brother. A lot of children would have been jealous, but she has a loving heart and she adored him. Then it was all taken away, mother, brother, the home life she'd known. She has to lash out at someone, and I'm the nearest, so I've become the biggest monster in creation. What am I supposed to have done?'

'Prevented Renata's mother taking her when she left,' Joanna said sympathetically.

Gustavo's lips twisted in mockery, perhaps of his ex-wife, perhaps of himself.

'Did Crystal plead with me to release her darling child, and I cruelly broke off all contact between them?'

'Something like that.'

'God, what a mess! Do I have to tell you that Crystal could have taken her if she'd wished, but she didn't? The clown she's living with doesn't want Renata hanging around, and Crystal didn't put up a fight. She dumped her daughter and left without a backward glance.

'She doesn't even keep in touch. She's supposed to call Renata, but she doesn't bother. If I call her she makes an excuse and hangs up.'

'I see,' she said slowly. 'It's just that Renata told me—'

'What? It's best if I know. What has the poor little soul told herself now?'

'She says Crystal bought her a cellphone and they talk every day.'

Gustavo dropped his head into his hands.

'She does have a cellphone,' he said at last. 'I bought it to help them stay in touch. And I can tell you, Crystal never calls on it. What's more, she keeps her own cellphone switched off, so Renata can't get through. I get the phone records sent to me every week so that I can tell what's happening.'

He gave a grunt of harsh laughter, then said with terrible bitterness, 'It would be nice if my child confided in me, but since she doesn't, the phone records keep me up-to-date.'

'Oh, heavens!' she breathed. 'I wish I knew what to say.'

'Saying things is useless. It doesn't make anything better. I found that out long ago.'

'And Renata blames you for all this?'

'Of course. It's that or admit that her mother doesn't want her. What is the poor little thing to do? I long to help her, but I seem to be the one person who can't. I'm floundering.'

He gave her a painful smile.

'This is quite like old times. Do you remember how I used to confide in you?'

She almost gave an exclamation of shock. He'd confided in her? Had he? She searched her brain for anything that could have given him such memories, but although she could remember long talks as they rode or walked together, she could recall nothing she would have described as personal confidences. And yet that was what he remembered.

'I know we talked a lot,' she said cautiously. 'Especially when we were here.'

'I used to enjoy those talks,' he said. 'I always felt that I could tell you everything I was thinking, and you would understand. I'd never felt that with anyone before. Or since.'

'But the things we talked about—' she stammered '—they were just—'

'It didn't matter what we talked about. Your mind was always there with mine. Or at least, that was what you made me feel. It was a good feeling.'

She was stunned. Had she been so absorbed by her own feelings that she'd failed to appreciate that Gustavo placed his own value on their relationship, a different one from hers?

For the first time it struck her that there had been something self-centred in her love. She'd fallen for Prince Charming, but she'd had no insight into the thoughts of the real man.

'Of course,' he added, 'years spent living with a woman who couldn't have cared less what I was thinking may have heightened my impression of you. Joanna, I can't tell you what it's like seeing you again. When Carlo told me he'd made an arrangement with Mrs Manton I had no idea it would be you.'

'And you're not sorry that it is?'

'Of course not. It's marvellous to me that we should have met again like this. I've thought of you so often through the years.'

Joanna turned a wry, disbelieving face towards him, making him ask, 'Why do you look at me like that?'

'I should think I'm the last person you'd want to remember.'

'Why? We had no quarrel. I have only the kindest memories of you. Unless you're referring to the fact that I behaved badly.'

'You didn't. You behaved honestly. And ending our engagement suited me too. You know that.'

'But not the way it happened, surely?'

'You mean with me looking like a jilted wallflower?' she teased. 'Come on! I was never that. You should have seen me dancing at your wedding?'

'Yes, I did. Dance after dance with the same man. Who was he, by the way? Nobody I asked seemed to know him.'

She was almost knocked breathless by the discovery that Gustavo had noticed her that day and enquired about her partner. She had thought him oblivious.

'He was a friend of a friend. He dropped a lot of names, and acted like he belonged there. That's his style, charming his way through life and being so convincing that nobody challenges him.'

'You talk as though you know him well.'

'His name is Freddy Manton,' she said with the air of a conjurer producing a rabbit from a hat.

'You mean—?'

'I married him.'

There was a slight clatter as he set his glass down sharply.

'Were you in love with him all the time? You jumped at the chance to break up with me because of him?'

'No way. That was our first meeting. After that I didn't see him again for a year. Then we bumped into each other again and things happened. It had nothing to do with what happened to you and me.'

'I see,' he said slowly, and she couldn't tell if he was glad or disappointed.

She drained her glass, and Gustavo immediately re-filled it for her.

'Careful,' she said. 'I don't want to get tipsy.'

'You won't. I remember what a good head you always had.'

She gave a crack of laughter. 'What a thing to be remembered for!'

'I remember everything,' he said quietly. 'Everything. Don't you?'

CHAPTER FOUR

DID she remember everything? she wondered. What about the things she'd tried so hard to blot out?

'Yes, I suppose I do,' she said.

'One thing that always puzzled me is why you ever let yourself be part of that merry-go-round.'

'Blame Aunt Lilian,' she said. 'She really belonged in the nineteenth century, when things were done that way. I suppose I just got on board and didn't know how to get off.'

'Until the last moment, when you jumped off in a panic. Forgive me, Joanna. I never realised that you were being forced.'

'It wasn't quite like that,' she said quickly.

'I wish I knew exactly how it was. After we broke up I wanted to talk to you before the wedding, but I didn't know what to say.'

'There was nothing. It had all been said.'

'Had it?' he asked in a low voice. 'Or could it never be said?'

'Both, of course. Look—' she set her glass down, leaned forward and gripped his hands '—what's the point of being wise all these years later? It's over. It happened. We're different people now.'

He nodded. 'It's strange. I once knew you so well, and now I know nothing about you.'

You're mistaken, she thought. You never knew the most important thing about me.

53

'I'm glad you married,' he said. 'I hope you had some good years before your divorce. You deserve the best.'

'That's nice of you.'

'I'm not just saying it. I still remember your generosity. If you only knew how much I admired you at that time. You were strong and I was—' he shrugged '—I just had to put myself in your hands.'

'And you hated that,' she said wryly.

'Now you make me sound churlish. But a man doesn't like to think of himself as hiding behind a woman's skirts like a weakling.'

'Does it make you a weakling to accept help? I was simply better placed to do the talking. Besides, isn't love supposed to make strong men weak? And heaven knows, you were madly in love with Crystal.'

'Yes,' he said solemnly.

She waited to see if he would say more, but a heaviness seemed to have come down on him.

She sat on the stone railing, raising one leg to rest her arm against the knee, and looked out over the scene.

Looking at her confused him. She was Joanna and yet not Joanna. The girl of long ago was still there, but only as a faint ghost. The woman of today had a glamour and confidence that girl had never dreamed of.

He'd watched her over dinner, fascinated by the way she had turned into a beauty, her light tan emphasising her large grey eyes and making her smile flash.

But it was more than that, more than the silk and velvet of her clothes or the real gold in her ears. She had made a success of her life, donning authority like a cloak and walking through the world with a superior air.

They called her 'Boss!' and it was only half a joke. She had earned the title, not inherited it. He felt at a disadvantage, and that brought a memory back.

'Do you remember the night you came out here before?' he asked.

'Maybe,' she said dreamily.

'I saw you here, sitting just where you are now, and I wanted to come and talk to you but you seemed so absorbed in your own world that I couldn't bear to disturb you.'

'Oh,' she said softly.

'I did come out in the end—but it was all wrong.'

'I remember that we didn't say much.'

'I had an odd feeling that you wanted to tell me something, but you never did, so I guess I was mistaken.'

She was silent, recalling that night and how awkward their conversation had been. How astute of him to have sensed that there were words she longed to say! How blind not to have realised that they were words of love!

From deep in the woods the owl hooted again.

'There was an owl that night too,' she said, smiling. 'That one's probably descended from it. Nothing ever really changes here, does it? That was one of the things I loved about the place.'

'Nothing changes,' he agreed. 'And everything changes.'

'Yes,' she said after a moment. 'Everything changes.'

Then, for a while, there was nothing more to say.

Joanna found herself pervaded by an unexpected sense of peace and contentment. She felt that she could sit here forever.

Gustavo remained in a chair, watching her as she looked out over the darkened landscape, her hair lifted by the slight breeze that was so welcome at the end of a hot day.

Once she turned her head towards him and smiled, but they did not speak. Time seemed to slip past without her noticing, and she was startled to see the first streaks of light in the sky.

'Is that the dawn?' she asked.

'Yes, but it's only about four o'clock.'

'That's right. I used to stand at my bedroom window and watch it happen. It was glorious.'

'I expect you were dreaming of the great lost palace even then,' he said with a smile.

She had been dreaming of him, and the life they would have together. But she only nodded.

'That palace has filled my dreams,' she agreed. 'Being the one to uncover it means everything to me. I remember the day you told me about it, and took me to the place where it was supposed to have stood, fifteen hundred years ago.'

'But that wasn't the right place, was it?' he said.

'According to all the books it should have been there. Only the real thing turned out to be about half a mile away. Carlo said it was found by chance, when some of the earth settled, leaving a dent in the ground.'

'That's right. I'm sorry I wasn't here when you arrived. I'd have liked to be the one to take you there, and see your face.'

'I probably looked like a child on Christmas Day.'

'Yes, that's what I'd have enjoyed. I remember you as always so cool and composed. It would be delightful to see you bouncing up and down with excitement.'

Suddenly he stirred.

'Let me take you there now, Joanna, before the rest of the world awakens.'

'All right,' she said eagerly.

It took him five minutes to bring his car around, and together they drove slowly over the gradually lightening land.

At last the site came into view, dim and silent in the soft grey morning. They got out and went to stand looking over it.

'It's a slow business,' she told him. 'It's only at this end that we've uncovered very much in the way of foundations. Over there it's still covered in grass. We have to take it slowly to make sure that we preserve as much as possible in good condition.'

'How many times have I walked or ridden over this piece of land, and never suspected?' he mused. 'It just looked like everywhere else, but now, if I'm lucky, it might be my salvation.'

'In what sense?'

'I have to repay my debt to Crystal. When we married she put a lot of money into this place. Now she wants it all back. Of course, she's entitled to it, so I have to raise the cash somehow.'

'Can you do that?'

'I've managed to pay part of what I owe her, which is keeping her quiet for a while. But I'm going to have to find a big lump sum quite soon.'

'It sounds as though things are pretty bad.'

'I'm not crying poverty. I live well, as you can see. Carlo has told me how much I'm paying for your services and I can find it because it's a good investment. But if you could manage to discover a solid gold vase, preferably two thousand years old, plus some proof that it once belonged to Julius Caesar, who received it from Cleopatra, I'd be very grateful.'

He spoke in a satirical voice and she guessed she didn't have to explain to him what a wild hope this was.

A moment later he confirmed it, saying, 'It's all right, it's only wishful thinking making me talk nonsense.'

'Not nonsense. Miracles do happen.'

'I know,' he said, so softly that she almost didn't hear.

'What was that?'

'Nothing,' he said hastily. 'Tell me, what's that I see over there? It looks like a whole village.'

'We travel with everything we need. One of those tents is a makeshift canteen.'

'And those trucks behind the tents?'

'Equipment, including a portable generator, that works the fridge in the canteen, so we can all have a nice cold beer. Independence is everything when you work all over the place, as we do.'

'That's another thing I recall about you, your independence. Be self-sufficient, and owe nothing to any man. That was your motto.'

'I'm sure I never said that.'

'You never had to. You were only eighteen, but even then, there was something about you that was complete unto yourself.'

'Then you were probably lucky not to marry me,' she said lightly. 'Self-sufficient people can be hell on earth to live with. They often know how to give but not to take, and that can be just as hurtful.'

'Well, it might make a change from someone who only knew how to take and never gave anything in her life,' he said with a touch of irony.

The next moment he hurriedly backed off.

'Please forget I said that. I make good resolutions not to criticise Crystal. It's sometimes hard to keep them, but she's still the mother of my child.'

'Of course. And as for what you were saying, I'm not sure you were right about me.'

'Well, I always wondered just how real your armour was. It was as though you'd told yourself to be that way, although I can't think why. Maybe you felt safer.'

She was about to protest when she remembered her vow never to love or feel again with the intensity with which she'd loved Gustavo. She'd opted for self-sufficiency then, but had the seeds of it already been there inside her heart long before? And had he sensed them, and drawn back from her?

She'd never thought of Gustavo as having insight. If anything, the reverse. Now, as he revealed her to herself, she wondered how well she'd ever really known him.

'Look,' he said suddenly, pointing upward.

The grey faded and a glow was appearing in the sky as the sun prepared to rise. Yet it was still early enough for a cool breeze.

'I always thought this the perfect time of day,' he said softly.

'Yes.'

He was standing a little behind her and she felt him put his hands gently on her shoulders. After that neither of them moved as they stood watching the light grow, until the sun blazed from behind a cloud and they had to shield their eyes.

'I suppose we'd better go back,' he said reluctantly.

On the journey home Joanna did not speak. Her inner vision was full of the glory she had seen, and the greater glory she had felt.

She was trying not to hear the little warning voice that had spoken before. It was more urgent now.

Go away from here, quickly. Leave before it's too late.

But it was already too late.

Business matters, both estate and financial, claimed Gustavo over the next few days. Several times he drove into Rome, always choosing a route that took him past the dig, fascinated by the way the area had become un-recognisable.

Sometimes he would stop off and let them show him around the other tents, which contained tables on which small pieces of brick and pottery were laid out.

He arrived one lunchtime, on his way back from the city, and saw Joanna, deep in discussion with Hal.

Stepping inside, he found the air pleasantly cool, courtesy of the portable air-conditioning system imported on one of the trucks.

'It's like an army on the move,' he said.

'That's down to Sally,' Joanna said.

Sally looked up long enough to intone, 'Logistics. The secret of a good campaign.'

'It shows how ignorant I am,' Gustavo said. 'I used to think it would be a couple of people with trowels.'

'I've got a trowel,' said Danny, who was by way of being the clown of the group.

'We use those too,' Joanna told him. 'But we also have radar, laser photography and computers. There's a mass of equipment in the trucks.'

Gustavo saw Billy in a corner, peering at the screen of a laptop and tapping something in with the ease of familiarity, and talking to Renata, who hung on to his every word. He watched them with satisfaction, and exchanged a glance with Joanna.

'Thank you,' he said quietly. 'He's just what she needs right now.'

'I think she's giving him something that he needs too,' she mused.

'Yes, I imagine hero-worship can be very heady wine when you're ten,' he agreed, smiling.

Casually he strolled over to the children, looking at the screen, asking about it. Billy answered cheerfully, and even Renata, Joanna was glad to notice, gave him a faint smile. When he spoke directly to her she began to explain something to him. Glad for him, Joanna edged discreetly forward.

'You're really learning about this fast,' Gustavo was saying to his daughter.

'Joanna says I'm good at it,' Renata told him solemnly.

'She is,' Joanna confirmed. 'She never has to be told anything twice.'

'Bright girl.' Gustavo smiled at his daughter. She smiled back at him, and for once there was no strain in her face.

Please, let it always be like this for him, Joanna thought.

Something was making Gustavo do everything right. He pointed at the screen, declared himself baffled and begged enlightenment. Renata was happy to oblige until she got stuck.

'No—wait— Billy, is that the right word?' she asked.

'No, you mean—hang on.' His cellphone had shrilled. Holding it up, he grinned at something that appeared on the screen. 'It's my dad,' he told them. 'He sends me bad jokes by text message, and boy, is that a really bad joke! In fact, my dad can think of worse bad jokes than anyone else's dad in the world.'

'I reckon I could manage a few,' Gustavo said quickly.

'Nah! Dad's the champion bad joker. Top of the class. I think he's even got a degree in it. Look at that!'

'What does it mean?' Renata asked, peering at the English words.

He explained, but she was still puzzled.

'I think it lost something in translation,' Gustavo said, touching her lightly on the shoulder.

'That's the trouble with really bad jokes,' Billy said

solemnly. 'When you try to explain them, they die a horrible death.'

'I'm sure you can think of one even worse to send
back,' Joanna observed. 'After all, he may be the master
bad joker, but you're not his son for nothing.'

'You bet!'

Billy began to key in letters with practised fingers, then
triumphantly transmitted the text. The answer came a moment later and made him yell with laughter.

'That is the worst joke ever,' he crowed.

'Don't let him get away with that,' Joanna said. 'You
can beat it.'

He did so, receiving a response almost at once. The
others crowded around, joining in with suggestions that
grew sillier and sillier, until they reached a riotous peak
of silliness, and everyone was laughing.

Everyone except Renata. At some moment she had
seen the contrast between Billy's experience and her own
silent phone. Her face stiffened as though she was fight-
ing back the tears with an effort.

Joanna met Gustavo's eyes, signalling a frantic message to him. He tried to draw the child close to him but
she pulled away as all the hostility, so briefly abated,
came flooding back. The next moment she'd dashed out
of the tent.

Gustavo made as if to follow her but Joanna shook her
head and he stopped, held back by an instinctive trust in
her as she went out to find Renata.

The little girl had jumped down into the dig and was
sitting with her back to a low wall that had just been
revealed. Her arms were folded on her knees, and her
head rested on them in an attitude of silent despair.

Joanna jumped down and went to sit beside her, touching her arm lightly.

'I'm sorry that upset you,' she said.

'It didn't, not really,' Renata said defiantly. 'It just reminded me how much I miss Mamma. She called this morning, to say how much she loved me, and plan our escape. It's going to be very soon, but you won't tell Papa, will you?'

'No, I won't tell him,' Joanna said softly.

There would be no need, she thought, sensing Gustavo approach and stand just out of sight.

'Because if he knew—' Renata's voice wobbled '—he'd try to stop me.'

'Perhaps that's because he loves you,' Joanna suggested. 'I think he loves you so much that he can't bear to do without you. Did you ever think of that?'

Renata shook her head vigorously.

'Well, perhaps you should. After all, think how lonely he must be! You're all he has left. How can you think of leaving him all alone in this great place?'

For a moment she thought she'd got through. Renata's face cleared for a moment, but then she said, 'But Papa made Mamma and little Toni go away. Why would he do that if he was going to be lonely?'

'I don't think it was quite like that. Perhaps you should ask him to talk to you about what happened.'

'But I try to talk to him. He just puts me off and won't tell me anything properly, so I know he's lying to me.'

'He's not lying. There are just some things he finds very difficult to talk about. He needs you to help him, and look after him.'

'Look after Papa?' Renata said in a tone of disbelief. 'He doesn't need anyone to look after him.'

'Oh, if you only knew how wrong you are!'

Renata jumped to her feet.

'I'm not, I'm not. I hate you, and I hate Papa. I hate everyone but Papa most. *I hate him, I hate him, I hate him!*'

She jumped up and ran away. Billy came out of the tent and started running after her.

'Not in this heat!' Joanna called.

'It's all right.' That was Hal, heading for the nearest truck. 'I'll catch them up and take them back to the house.'

'Thanks, Hal.' She went to the tent entrance. 'Everyone back to the house for lunch.'

As she'd hoped they jumped at her suggestion. The next moment the cars were roaring away towards the house, leaving Joanna and Gustavo alone.

He had walked a little way off, stopping beneath the shade of a tree, his back to her. She could only imagine the agony this must be for him. To hear the child he loved more than anything in the world scream that she hated him. Could there be any pain greater?

Torn with sympathy for him, she walked up and touched him gently on the shoulder.

'It doesn't mean anything, Gustavo. All children say these things.'

'Yes,' he said, not turning round. 'They say them in tantrums about trivial things, but this wasn't trivial. Her heart is breaking, and she meant every word.'

Then he looked round, and she could clearly see that he had been weeping. He was past trying to hide it. The tears were still on his cheeks.

'Thank you for what you tried to do,' he said huskily.

'You know I'll help you all I can, Gustavo, but I don't understand. Where does Renata get this fixation from?'

'When Crystal walked out Renata saw her leaving and came flying downstairs, trying to hold on to her. Crystal said she'd send for her "later" and got into the car. Renata tried to get in with her, and that was when I grabbed her, to stop her getting hurt.'

'So that's the origin of the story of you keeping her away from Crystal?'

'Yes. I'm not sure she even remembers the reality any more. I'm the monster who snatched her from her mother's arms, and she's told herself that so often that it's become "fact". Crystal never did send for her, and this is the only way she can cope with it.'

'I'll talk to her again when she's calmed down,' Joanna promised. 'Or maybe I'll route some of it through Billy. She might listen to him.'

He tried to smile and speak normally.

'I'm lucky to have you two here, because without you I don't…' But it was too much. The next moment he broke.

'What am I going to do?' he whispered. 'Help me, Joanna. I've nobody else to turn to. *Help me!*'

She put her arms around him, holding him consolingly, feeling him cling to her tightly, desperately.

'My dear, of course I will. I'll do anything I can. Hold on to me. It'll be all right, you'll see. I promise it's going to be all right.'

CHAPTER FIVE

WHEN evening came Joanna didn't go back to the house for dinner, but stayed at the dig while the sun set. More than anything she wanted to be alone now. The events of the day had shaken her.

She'd come to Montegiano prepared to fight off any renewal of the old passionate feelings. What she hadn't anticipated was finding him wounded, so that her heart yearned towards him in sympathy. That would be harder to resist. Perhaps impossible.

She looked up as she heard his car approach. She'd wondered if he would come seeking her, and decided that he probably would not. The moment when he'd come into her arms seeking comfort had not lasted. Afterwards he had been edgy, nervous, insisting on driving her back to the house for lunch. That was another reason why she had avoided dinner that evening.

As he got out of the car he was smiling as though everything was normal, and she realised that he was determined to act as if nothing had happened. He was probably ashamed that she'd seen his 'weakness', she thought wryly.

'I brought you some food,' he said. 'They told me you weren't at supper.'

So he hadn't been there either.

'Thanks,' she said, 'but you didn't have to bother. I've had a sandwich and I've got a beer.' She waved the can.

'That's not enough for someone working long hours

in the heat,' he said, unwrapping some chicken for her. 'You'll be ill if you don't take care.'

'I'm invulnerable,' she said lightly. 'Nothing ever hurts me.'

'It's people who talk that kind of nonsense who get hurt,' he informed her. 'You should have more common sense.'

'Oh, stuff! I was always famous for my common sense. People used to say of me "She may be as dull as ditch-water but you've got to admit she has common sense".'

'Then I guess you lost your common sense when you stopped being dull,' he said. 'Except that you never were.'

'Didn't I bore your head off, talking history all the time?'

'Nobody bores me by talking about my home,' he said. 'Even then I was impressed by your knowledge.'

'But we were supposed to be a courting couple,' she reminded him, teasing. 'And there we were, talking about Julius Caesar.'

'It wasn't always Julius Caesar.'

'That's right. We touched on Lucrezia Borgia as well. There's something not quite right about that, if only I could put my finger on it.'

He joined in her laughter. They had slipped back into their usual way of talking, which, she guessed, was what he'd wanted.

She put the beer can to her lips, throwing her head back and draining it like a man, finishing with a sigh of pleasure.

'You've got foam on your mouth,' he said, taking out a clean handkerchief.

'Thank you.' She stood quietly until he'd finished dabbing her lips.

'I don't think you take proper care of yourself,' he said.

'I don't need to fuss about myself. I have everything I want. Look.' She indicated the half-revealed foundations stretching away from them.

As she said it a different look came over her face, as though she could see something that was hidden from him.

'Joanna,' he said uncertainly.

She touched his hand and moved away slowly, descending the few shallow steps that led down to where the foundations were beginning to show, and even some tiles. As he watched she dropped to her knees and ran her fingertips over the tiles, where the outline of a pattern was just visible.

Then she stood up and looked out over the whole dig, stretching over most of an acre, her face blazing with pride. She did not speak, but she didn't need to. She couldn't have said more clearly, This is my kingdom.

'Joanna,' he said softly.

When she did not seem to hear him he took hold of her shoulders and turned her towards him.

'Joanna,' he said again, giving her a little shake. 'Where are you?'

She gave him a smile, but there was something dreamy about it.

'I'm here,' she assured him.

'I don't think so. Sometimes I think the real world isn't very real to you at all.'

'You think this is the only real world?' she asked in surprise. 'Isn't the past real? It should be to you of all people. I thought you understood the excitement of passing into another universe where the rules are different.'

'But not more real than the present,' he said with a

touch of urgency, for the hairs were beginning to stand up on the back of his neck at a kind of strangeness that had come over her.

'It's like travelling, exploring wondrous places. It's the greatest excitement there is.'

'I think your world is inhabited by some very strange creatures. It's alarming.' He searched her face. 'You're a little alarming yourself.'

She looked up at him, smiling. The glow of the sun was on her face. Hardly knowing what he did, or why, he drew her hat off, so that the sun touched her hair too, seeming to turn her to gold. The sight of her held him still.

Joanna could not have moved if her life had depended on it. Gustavo was looking at her as he had never done before, as though she had his whole attention, even without his will. His expression was startled, unguarded, almost defenceless, and she knew that, for the second time that day, she had broken through to some inner place that had always been barred to her in the past.

She was flooded with warmth, although whether from the sun or from some other cause she did not know. She only knew that it was beautiful and sweet, and she wanted it to last forever.

'Joanna—' he whispered again.

The shrilling sound from her pocket seemed to go through them both, breaking the spell.

'What's that?' he asked tensely.

'My cellphone,' she groaned, pulling it out and answering it.

'Jo? This is Etta.'

'Who?' Her mind was blank.

'"Who?" she says! Henrietta Rannley, your second

cousin once removed. I'm calling from England. Now do you remember me?'

'Of course,' Joanna said, trying to pull herself together.

Etta was the daughter of Lord Rannley, the earl whose stately home had been the background for the drama twelve years ago. Then a child, she'd been Crystal's bridesmaid.

For a moment Joanna had to struggle to remember all this, because after the last few minutes Etta seemed as distant as though she were on another planet.

'I've been waiting to hear from you,' Etta said reproachfully.

'I'm sorry—about what?'

'About my wedding, of course. Are you coming or not? You were supposed to let me know.'

'Oh, heavens! Etta, I'm sorry, I really am—'

'But you got involved with some old bones so of course they came first.' She sounded amused. Like all Joanna's friends and relatives, she had learned to be tolerant.

'It wasn't like that—' Joanna began helplessly.

'Yes, it was. I know you. Anyway, can you tear yourself away for a couple of days?'

'I don't know. I'll try.'

'Good. I'll put you down as a definite.'

Joanna hung up, to find that Gustavo had walked away. It might have been simply courtesy, leaving her alone with her call, but she knew that for him the moment was over, and whatever it might have meant was gone.

Whatever it might have meant.

But something in her rebelled at the thought of going down that path again. She was no lovesick girl, to succumb easily to the sweet, dangerous magic. If she was wise she would escape this place while she could. A few days away would help her get everything in perspective.

'I think I'd like to go back to the house after all,' she said, joining him. 'I need a proper meal.'

'Of course,' he said politely. 'Let me drive you.'

On the way she began talking about indifferent things, and by the time they reached the house she had almost persuaded herself that she'd imagined it.

Over the next few days she wavered about whether to go back to England for the wedding. She told herself that she was needed here, although she knew her expert team could manage without her for a week, as they had done many times before.

Gustavo began spending more and more time at the dig, watching details emerge, as intently as though his salvation depended on it. Which in some ways it did, Joanna realised. It hurt her to see the tension in him, and to know that his dearest hopes were unlikely to be realised. To her this place was rich with history, but it was unlikely to bring him the hard cash he needed.

'It's not really like you read in books, is it?' he said to her one day. 'You dig up a brooch and it's worth a fortune.'

'We aren't likely to be finding things like that,' she told him gently. 'This is tiles and bricks.'

'Dull stuff.'

'To outsiders, yes.'

'No ancient remains? No valuable coins?'

'I'd find them for you if I could, but mostly it doesn't work like that.'

'I guess not. I'm sorry, Joanna. Take no notice of me. You have your job to do, and I'm not making it any easier.'

If she could only put her arms around him, and promise to find something that would make everything all right. The longing to do that swept over her with startling force, showing her the dangerous knife edge on which she was walking.

Abruptly she got up and walked away.

But almost at once there was a blinding flash.

'Was that lightning?' Hal asked, realising how sharply the temperature had dropped.

'I think it was,' Joanna said, her words almost drowned out by a crash of thunder.

'We get violent summer storms sometimes,' Gustavo said. 'Best get out of here quickly.'

But it was already too late. The next moment the heavens opened and rain poured down in sheets, soaking everyone at once, turning the soft ground into mud. After the heat there was a certain pleasure in simply standing there, pounded by cool rain. Joanna looked up to the sky, raising her arms in almost ecstatic welcome.

People were trying to reach the edge of the dig and make for the refuge of the cars, but they slipped and slid around, clinging on to each other, laughing.

With their hair plastered to their heads nobody looked like themselves any more. Sodden clothes became transparent, revealing that some of the women were naked beneath their shirts. They clutched their arms across their chests while the young men competed to assist them.

'Are you all right?' Gustavo called to Joanna.

'It's in my eyes; I can't see. Oh, heavens!'

She reached out and he took hold of her arm, shouting through the din, 'Hold on to me.'

She clutched wildly and felt his arms go around her just as her foot gave way in the mud. Floundering, she seized him, but her hands slipped on his sodden shirt and she had to grasp hard.

She had the sensation of a hard, muscular body beneath her palms. It belonged to a stranger. The young Gustavo had kissed her with restraint and she'd forced herself to respond in kind, her arms demurely about his neck. She hadn't dared yield to the impulse to run her hands over him, the way she seemed to be doing now.

It was a startling discovery, almost like touching him for the very first time. This was a man who concealed power beneath expensive clothes.

'Are you all right?' came his voice in her ear.

'I think so,' she said through the pounding water.

With one hand she was holding on to his arm, while her other was about his neck. And he was laughing. She could feel it along his arm, then her arms, and deep in his chest, pressed against hers. It seemed to go through her again and again, and she answered it with her own laughter, melting into his, so that there was no knowing where he ended and she began. And all the time she couldn't see him.

'One step at a time,' he said. 'Careful.'

She moved gingerly forward, one step, then two.

'I can't see where I'm going,' she cried.

'It doesn't matter. I'm holding you.'

'But how can you see?'

'I can't,' he shouted cheerfully. 'But sooner or later— *Hey!*'

The last word was a yell as his foot slid out from under him, so that he had no choice but to go down into the mud, taking Joanna with him, still clasped in his arms. She landed on top of him and they lay there, helpless with laughter.

The others, seeing what was happening, surged back

to rescue them. Hands reached out and hauled them both up.

At last she managed to get her eyes clear and look around. Gustavo was sitting on the edge of the shallow bank, wiping his eyes and trying to brush his hair back.

He was covered in mud. It soaked his clothes so that they clung to him, revealing every line of his body. Now she could clearly see what she had only sensed before. His body was perfectly proportioned without an extra ounce anywhere. His sodden trousers clung to him so closely that he might as well have been naked.

Looking down, she saw that the same was true of her. Her breasts were outlined in vivid detail. She reckoned she must be light-headed because it was suddenly clear to her why female wrestlers used mud and why men cheered them on. But Gustavo wasn't cheering. He looked astounded.

Another flash of lightning announced an even harder downpour. In seconds everyone was in vehicles heading back to the house. Joanna travelled with Gustavo but his attention was taken up with the road, which seemed to slip and slide away from the car.

Once inside they all headed for their bedrooms to dive under showers with cries of pleasure and relief. Joanna let the hot water lave over her, feeling good as the mud drained away, followed by soapsuds. But she was acting mechanically. With her eyes closed again, she was playing back what she had seen, playing it over and over, relishing every moment.

She had forgotten that Gustavo came from a line of princes, men who had lived in splendour while ruling 'their' people ruthlessly. To the world they presented an appearance of elegance. You had to get close to sense the leashed power, even menace, that lay beneath.

It almost made her laugh out loud to think that an accident had revealed more of his body than she had learned as his fiancée. But it had come years too late, when there could no longer be anything between them.

Then her laughter died.

She switched off the water and stepped out, wrapping herself in towels. Slowly she went to sit on the huge bed with its ornate painted bedhead.

Inside her head she lived it all again, the feel of him against her, firm and vibrant. And responding to her, as aware of her as she was of him. There had been no mistaking the look on his face. He'd been thunderstruck. Just as she had been.

What was he doing now? Sitting in his own room, thinking thoughts that echoed her own? Was he, too, filled with alarm? Or had it meant nothing, a brief flash of desire that had flared and gone?

Or perhaps lingered, as it had lingered with her?

She would know something when she saw him at supper. It would be there in his eyes, in the way he stood, in the sound of his voice when he spoke to her.

But when she went down Carlo said that Gustavo wouldn't be joining them tonight. He'd received an urgent summons from a business acquaintance in Rome, and would be gone for several hours.

Joanna smiled and said that she understood how many calls on the prince's time there must be.

But inwardly she whispered, Now I know all that I need to. I promised myself I wouldn't let it happen again. It's over. *It's over!*

Later that night she slipped into her son's room.

'Billy, would you mind if I went away for a few days?'

'Nope. Don't suppose I'll even know you're gone,' he said with a grin.

She flicked his hair. 'Watch it, cheeky!'

'Honest, Mum, now I've started riding, I'm having a great time. Besides,' he added, 'I think Renata copes better when I'm there.'

Joanna nodded. 'I think so too. I'll be a week. Tops.'

He regarded her satirically. 'Have you got a boyfriend?'

'No, I'm going to Etta's wedding, and if I have any more lip out of you I'll make you come with me. She did once ask if you could be a pageboy—'

'I'll be good, I'll be good,' he said, holding up his hands in a theatrical gesture of prayer.

She laughed and kissed him goodnight. But as she turned away she remembered something.

'Do you know how Gustavo is managing with Renata now?'

'Not well,' he said. 'I heard him talking to her yesterday. He started well enough, trying to be nice and all that. But he ended up telling her she'd do as she was told.'

'Oh, give me patience,' Joanna groaned. 'He means well. He really isn't the monster you thought, Billy.'

'I know. Like you say, he does his best, but he doesn't seem to know the right things to say.'

'That sounds like him. Goodnight, darling.'

She slept little that night, trying to silence the voice that said it wasn't too late to change her mind. She could abandon her trip and stay here.

At last she pulled herself together. If the prospect of a few days away could reduce her to a nervous wreck, then it was time she left.

Next morning she talked to Laura, who was totally

under Billy's spell and promised to take good care of him. Carlo promised the same thing.

'Great kid,' he said. 'Don't worry. I'll try to keep him out of mischief, and if I fail I'll make sure you never find out.'

'It sounds like you've got it well sussed. I'd better speak to Gustavo now.'

'I'm afraid he isn't back yet.'

'You mean—not back from last night?'

'That's right. He does this occasionally. If it's been a very good dinner he wouldn't want to drive home.'

'No, of course not.'

'And sometimes there might be another reason,' Carlo said delicately.

For a moment she didn't understand. 'Another reason?'

'Well, his wife has been gone for some months now, and Rome is full of attractive ladies who don't ask for commitment. You could hardly blame him—'

'Yes, I see what you mean,' she said hastily. 'Fine, I'll catch him later.'

She left him before he could tell her any more and went to her room, cursing herself for her own stupidity. Where had her wits been wandering?

She threw some clothes into a bag, then went out to the dig and spent an hour talking with her team, who, as she'd known, were cheerfully unfazed by the thought of managing without her.

Suddenly she saw Gustavo's car approaching and waited for him to stop as he'd often done before. But he drove past. There was nothing for it but to follow him.

She reached the house about ten minutes later and went to look for him in his study. Like the rest of the house it was awesomely impressive, with shelves of books climbing to the ceiling.

He looked up when she entered and smiled briefly, but she had the impression that he was no more relaxed than herself.

'I've come to say that I'm going to England for a few days,' she said.

He stared. 'What did you say?'

'I need to check some things in the British Museum.'

She was planning to do that as well. It seemed more tactful to say nothing about a wedding.

He set down the paper he had been holding and stared at her.

'I don't understand.' His voice was curt.

'I'm going to England for a few days.'

'Nonsense,' he said sharply. 'There can be no need for that.'

Informing Gustavo should have been no more than a formality. Opposition was the last thing she had expected, and it had the effect of making her stubborn.

'I think I'm the best judge of the necessity,' she said coolly.

'You have duties here.'

'I'm aware of my responsibilities here, but you must leave it to me to decide how best to fulfil them.'

'And your team? How will they manage?'

'If my team couldn't work on their own they wouldn't be my team.'

Gustavo's eyes became harder and obstinate lines appeared around his mouth.

'Surely you'd do better to consult Italian museums?'

'There are things I can only find in the British Museum.'

'This is not a good idea,' he said curtly. 'I would prefer you not to go.'

Joanna regarded him with her head on one side. Gustavo

was normally so punctilious that the sight of him growing angry was astonishing.

'Gustavo,' she said very gently, 'I'm not asking your permission.'

'Perhaps you should, since I'm employing you.'

She drew a deep breath and answered with restraint.

'Even if you were employing me, it wouldn't mean you controlled how I spend every moment of my time.'

'What do you mean "even *if*"?'

'Strictly speaking, you're employing Manton Research, and I work for the firm. The only person entitled to give me orders is the managing director.'

'And who is that?'

'Well, it's me, actually, but—'

'In that case, Madam Managing Director, I have a complaint to make about one of your employees, a lady who seems to think she can do her job at long distance. I am paying your firm for her services and I expect you to provide them.'

Joanna's voice was tight.

'If Your Excellency would care to study the contract you signed, you will see that all such decisions are the prerogative of the managing director. I and I alone shall decide the best use of Mrs Manton's time.'

'Mrs Manton has barely arrived and does not have my permission to leave.'

'Mrs Manton has *my* permission to leave, and does not need yours.'

'Then I can only say that I consider her thoroughly unprofessional, and I suggest she thinks about that.'

Joanna stared at him, trying to get her bearings. This wasn't the Gustavo she'd thought she knew, but a hasty, arrogant man who presumed to judge her.

It crossed her mind that if she'd been leaving to avoid

reigniting her old feelings, then she need no longer bother. Just being in Gustavo's company would protect her very nicely.

But she was in too much of a temper to give in now, and Gustavo's own temper was reaching new heights.

'Is this how your firm normally works?' he demanded cuttingly. 'Takes on a job, does it for a few weeks, then the head of the team vanishes and leaves the rest of the work to the underlings? I suppose there's another job waiting for you, and you'll run the two in tandem. Well, let me make it clear that I won't tolerate—'

'How *dare* you!' she raged. 'You ought to be ashamed of yourself, saying such a thing to me.'

He had the grace to become uneasy.

'All right,' he snapped. 'I went too far.'

'Much too far,' she snapped back.

'I retract my words, but not my opposition. How do I know you'll come back?'

'Because I'm a woman of my word,' she said indignantly. 'When I take on a job, I complete it. When I say I'll do something, I do it, and what I say now is that I am going to England.'

'If you do, you do so in opposition to my wishes.'

'I'll live with that,' she flung at him, and walked out before he could reply.

CHAPTER SIX

SHE saw Billy as she was crossing the hall and beckoned him to follow her upstairs to his room.

'Sorry, darling,' she said when they were inside. 'Change of plan. You're coming with me.'

'I'm not going to be a pageboy,' he said, looking around wildly.

'All right, it's a deal. Now go and chuck a few things into a bag.'

'But you said it was all right for me to stay here.'

'Not any more.'

She went to her own room and began to pack hurriedly, growing more enraged with every moment. Gustavo's refusal to be reasonable, as much as his haughtiness, had stunned her.

The knock at her door was tentative, even slightly nervous. Still seething, she yanked it open.

Gustavo was standing there. 'May I come in?'

She stood back for him to pass, and closed the door behind him.

'Are you still speaking to me?' he asked.

'Just about.'

'I suppose it's more than I deserve. Joanna, please forgive my ill-temper. I don't know what got into me. Of course you must go, if—if you think it's necessary.'

In the face of his contrition her anger died. She faced him, arms akimbo, her face full of fond exasperation.

'How could you believe that I wouldn't come back?'

'It sounds crazy, I know. It's just that what's happening out there is so important to me, and naturally it matters that the boss should be there.'

He sounded self-conscious, like a man hiding his true thoughts. Joanna wouldn't allow herself to speculate on what those thoughts might be.

'Mum,' Billy said, bursting in, 'do I need to pack my—?' He stopped, seeing Gustavo.

'You too?' Gustavo said quickly. 'But you surely don't want to leave just when you're beginning to ride so well?'

'I was originally hoping to leave Billy here,' Joanna said. 'But then—'

'And I hope you will,' Gustavo said. 'You know he'll be all right, and Renata would be lonely without him.'

'That would be better,' Joanna admitted. 'Thank you. It's all right, Billy, you can unpack.'

'But you just told me to pack.'

'Well, now you're staying, so you can unpack.'

In silence, Billy looked from one to the other, and tapped his forehead.

By late that evening Joanna was in London, installed in the Ritz, desperately relieved to have got away from Gustavo.

His contrition had been welcome, but it hadn't wiped out the memory of their quarrel when she'd seen a side of him that had shocked her—a man who demanded his own way as a right, who could be coldly autocratic to anyone who dared defy him.

She supposed it was inevitable in his position, but it was new to her, and it made her realise that she'd had a lucky escape.

She really would like to consult the British Museum, although it was perhaps less urgent than she'd made it sound. She spent three days there, hard at work. Every evening she called Billy, ready to return at once if he seemed less than happy. But his cheerful voice always reassured her.

'How is Gustavo?' she asked politely on the third evening.

'He's a bit worked up at the moment,' Billy observed. 'I think he's got shares in an airline.'

'Shares in an…? Billy, what are you talking about?'

'They're all on strike. Every airport in the country is closed down.'

'Oh, yes, I think I saw something on the news last night. Poor Gustavo. He does have bad luck. Is he around for me to talk to?'

'No, he's out for the evening.'

'Oh, well, it doesn't matter.'

For the evening or for the night? she wondered as she hung up.

But it was no concern of hers.

The following afternoon she returned to the hotel, hot, tired and eager for a shower. A strand of hair flopped over her forehead and she knew she looked far from her best. As she collected her messages the receptionist said, 'There's a gentleman waiting to see you.'

In the heartbeat before she turned to see him Joanna knew who she wanted it to be more than anyone in the world.

He had risen as she came in, and stood quietly watching her, an uncertain smile on his face. Joanna walked towards him, passionately glad to see him.

'I don't understand,' she said. 'How do you come to be here?'

'I happened to have business in London.'

'What a coincidence that we should both stay here.'

He shrugged. 'I always stay here, and I guessed that you might, so I asked at the desk.'

'So the airports are open again?'

'I've no idea. They were closed yesterday, so I took the train.'

'All that way by train? Why, it must take—'

'Twenty-eight hours.'

'Your business must be very urgent.'

He nodded, not taking his eyes from her. 'Yes,' he said quietly. 'It is.'

She made no answer. It mattered too much for words.

A sudden awkwardness overtook them both. The moment wasn't right.

He glanced at the books she was carrying. 'From the museum?'

'Yes, I treated myself in the museum shop.'

'They look heavy. May I carry them up for you?'

She relinquished them to him. Together they went to the lift, then up to her suite.

'I need a drink,' she said, kicking off her shoes. 'Who'd think you could get so tired just looking at manuscripts?'

'Paperwork,' he agreed. 'Guaranteed to give you a headache.'

They were talking about nothing to gain time and space. Now that their first greeting was over she was disconcerted at the sight of him. This wasn't the man whose body she'd clasped through the mud, or the arrogant autocrat who had antagonised her. He looked desperately weary, like someone who'd already absorbed too many blows and was tensed for more. He confirmed it when she asked what he wanted to drink and he asked for a whisky, which she'd never seen him with before.

He downed it in one and said heavily, 'I lied to you. I knew you were here. I asked Billy.'

'He didn't tell me that.'

'I swore him to secrecy. I said I wanted to surprise you, and he mustn't spoil it.'

'I'll bet he loved that, the little monkey.'

'Yes, he did. I envy you. What a son to have!'

She remembered that his own son wasn't his son at all, but couldn't think of anything to say that wouldn't sound insultingly trivial.

'Another drink?' she asked gently.

'Perhaps I shouldn't. I'm going to ask you to dinner, so I'd better keep a clear head.'

'Like I'm an ogre?' she said lightly. 'Forget it. We'll eat here and I'll be the host.'

'Thank you.' He held out his glass and she poured him another whisky.

'I lied about having business too,' he admitted. 'I just followed you. I couldn't bear it that you went away angry with me, even though I deserved it.'

'I wasn't angry—' she began, but he interrupted her quickly.

'Yes, you were, and you were right. I behaved abominably.'

'I don't think you were abominable,' she said, although she'd been thinking exactly that. 'I was just a bit surprised. I've never seen you like that before.'

He smiled faintly. 'I didn't want you to go and I couldn't think of any other way to say it. I'm afraid I tend to fall back on barking out orders when—when I feel at a disadvantage. I shouldn't have acted that way, with you of all people.'

'You don't owe me anything.'

'We both know what I owe you, but—let's talk about

that later. First tell me why you suddenly decided to leave Montegiano.'

'I told you—'

'Yes, yes, you told me some neat story about working in the British Museum.'

'I've really been to the British Museum, and I've discovered some fascinating—'

'Joanna, can we please forget about old ruins for a while, even my old ruins? Right now they don't seem very important.'

'I never thought to hear you say that.'

'Neither did I, but sometimes… Did you leave to get away from me?'

'How—exactly—do you mean that?' she asked cautiously.

'Do I make things too difficult for you—because of the past?'

'What past? We were friends. We're still friends. End of story. Look, I knew whose home it was when I went there. I wasn't taken by surprise. I just thought it would be nice to see how you were.'

'But you didn't expect to find me alone. Perhaps if you'd known that, you wouldn't have come.'

'Why should you say that?'

'Because I wonder if you found our meeting awkward.'

'After all these years? We're not the same people that we were then.'

'True,' he said, looking into his glass. 'The years do their work. They give and they take away. They show us the lessons to be learned, and those lessons change us, so that we look back and don't recognise ourselves as we were then.'

'Would you go back to being the man you were then?' she asked.

He shook his head. 'At twenty-two I wasn't even a man. Just a callow boy who thought he knew it all because he'd been raised in a privileged position. What a fool! I fell for the first fairy tale that was fed to me. A man with a shred of experience or worldly wisdom would have seen through her.'

'Was it really as bad as that?' she asked sympathetically.

He nodded.

'I thought I'd arrive to see you and Crystal together in domestic bliss.'

'Domestic bliss,' he said wryly. 'It was never that.'

'It didn't occur to me that things might have gone wrong, especially after I read in the papers about your son being born.'

He winced. 'Yes, there was a proper announcement about a son and heir being born to the Prince of Montegiano. But you should have seen what the papers made of the other juicy little item, when the boy turned out to be the son and heir of the princess's fitness instructor.'

She heard the pain in his voice, and saw it in his twisted smile. How much was wounded love for a woman who had betrayed him? she wondered. And how much was humiliation, because the world knew he was a cuckold?

Did it matter? Whatever the truth, his misery was intense.

'Let's have some dinner,' she said briskly. 'Everything looks better on a full stomach.' She handed him the room-service menu. 'I feel like a feast.'

She was afraid that he might demur at the idea of her

treating him, but he simply looked contented. When the feast was chosen she said, with a twinkle, 'I'll leave the wines to you.'

'Tactful lady!'

'Well, I'm not going to risk choosing wines for an Italian, and a Roman at that.'

'Not only tactful but also wise.'

'We'll do it properly,' she said. 'A different wine with every course. And champagne.'

'Champagne?'

Just having him here was a cause for celebration, but she couldn't say that so she just gave a private smile of happiness.

When the meal arrived they gave it all their attention for a while. Gustavo said little, but now and then he glanced across at her, as though making sure that she was still there.

After a while, when it seemed to her that he was more relaxed, Joanna said gently, 'What happened?'

'What happened was that I made the biggest mistake any man has ever made,' he said slowly. 'I gave my whole heart and soul to a woman who had no heart to give back. She fed me a line and I fell for it.'

'But she was crazy about you. I saw you together.'

He shook his head. 'No, she wanted me to be crazy about her. It's not the same thing. And she knew how to make me crazy. It was the title. She fancied being a princess. She as good as admitted it eventually.'

'How long did it take you to see the truth?'

'Much longer than it should have done. I couldn't let myself admit that she was greedy, selfish and cold. Which probably makes me a coward.'

His voice was sharp with bitterness and self-mockery.

'Don't be so hard on yourself,' Joanna urged.

'Why not? Someone should be hard on me for being such a fool. And with you I can be honest because you know the truth that nobody else knows.'

She gazed at him, shocked that everything she had tried to do for him had come to this.

'But it wasn't your fault. You wouldn't be the first man in the world to be taken in.'

'No, but—here's the joke—I considered myself being above that sort of thing. After all, I was a Montegiano, a man of pride and position.'

He gave a gruff laugh. 'Joanna, you have no idea of the stupidity of a boy of twenty-two who's been raised to think too well of himself. He makes mistake after mistake. The merest country bumpkin would have known better than I did.'

She held her breath, knowing what it must cost him to reveal himself like this, praying not to spoil everything by a clumsy word.

'You've really been through the mill, haven't you?' she asked.

He shrugged.

'Don't you have friends you can talk to?'

'There's nobody I can admit all this to, the way I can to you. You're the only person in the world who could understand because you saw things nobody else saw. We haven't seen each other for twelve years, yet in an odd way you know me better than anyone alive.'

He passed his hand over his eyes.

'Perhaps that's why I came running after you. I need to be with you, talk to you, even lean on you. That isn't very dignified, I know—'

'Why does it have to be dignified?' she said urgently. 'Why can't you ask for my help if you need it? I'm your friend, Gustavo, and if my friendship can help you then it's there.'

She took his hand. 'Talk to me, Gustavo. Tell me all the things you've been hiding away under that tightly buttoned-down exterior of yours. Because if you don't let them out soon, you'll go crazy.'

Joanna had a sudden sense of standing at a crossroads, of being given back the chance she'd overlooked years ago: the chance to be the friend he badly needed.

It wasn't love. It might even stand in the way of love. But it was what he craved from her, and she would not fail him.

'Tell me,' she said softly. 'When did it start to go wrong? You were so happy at first.'

'At first I thought I'd landed in heaven. She seemed the perfect wife, beautiful, loving, always looking for ways to please me. My vanity was so colossal that I accepted that as natural.'

'Why shouldn't you?' she burst out indignantly. It hurt her to hear him put himself down. 'If you love someone you do want to please them, because when they're happy, you're happy. Wasn't it that way with you too?'

'Yes,' he said. 'I loved finding ways to give her pleasure. That's why we went to Las Vegas. All I wanted was some quiet place where I could be alone with her, but she didn't like quiet places. She wanted excitement. I always knew we were different in that way, but I thought the love would help us overcome that.'

'But it didn't?'

'How can it when it's all on one side?' he asked quietly.

'But she did love you once.'

'Did she? Even now I wish I could believe it. I suppose

she loved me well enough when she got her own way, but I started to realise that I was always the one to yield.

'For a while even that didn't matter. She got pregnant and I was thrilled. Yes, I wanted a son, I don't deny it. And when it was a girl, I was disappointed—for about five minutes. Then I saw how gorgeous she was and I forgot all about wanting a son.

'As she grew older I loved her more, because she's so like my mother. She looks like her, she has her mental sharpness, and her stubbornness.' He gave a wry laugh. 'Mamma also saw the world in her own way, and you could point out the facts until you were blue in the face.'

'But Renata's a child,' Joanna reminded him. 'She'll understand in time.'

'You wouldn't say that if you'd known Mamma.'

'I did. Well, I met her briefly.'

'Yes, she liked you a lot. She was furious with me for letting you go.' He gave a brief laugh. 'If you could have heard what she called me.'

Joanna laughed. 'And you took no notice because you're as stubborn as her. The line passes from her to Renata through you.'

'Yes,' he admitted ruefully. 'And it makes me wonder if Renata will ever turn back to me. There's something implacable about her that makes me afraid.'

'Was Renata close to Crystal?'

'She wanted to be. She longed to be pretty like her mother, and Crystal would have liked a daughter who looked like a dainty fairy, which Renata doesn't.'

'She's better than that,' Joanna said at once. 'Her looks are going to be striking when she grows up.'

'That's what I think,' he said eagerly. 'But Crystal couldn't see it. She lost interest. The poor little kid was always trying to get her mother's attention, always wondering why she couldn't have it.'

'It sounds to me as if her fantasies started right back then,' Joanna mused.

'How do you mean?'

'We all tell each other fairy tales to cope with the pain of rejection,' she said, not looking at him. 'Renata invented another Crystal, one who was proud of her and wanted to be with her. In her mother's presence she had to face the reality, but when she was alone she could believe the fairy-tale version. Now Crystal's gone that version has taken over, but it actually began long ago.'

'Of course it did,' Gustavo said, looking at her quickly. 'Why didn't I see it before?'

'You were too close, and you have that pain to cope with as well.'

'Renata's rejection. Yes. But what can I do?'

'Be patient. She'll choose the time. There's no other way.'

'I know,' he sighed. 'I know you're right, it's just—'

'It's just that you're not the most patient man in the world,' she said sympathetically. 'I know.'

She poured him some more wine, and he drank it.

'So Crystal wasn't happy,' Joanna said, to encourage him to continue.

'No, I think she felt fairly soon that she'd made a mistake. I think that's my fault for marrying her in such haste. I should have brought her to Montegiano first so that she could see for herself whether the life would suit her. But I wanted her so much that I just grabbed the chance. We might both have been saved a lot of grief if I hadn't.

'She was bored with the estate, bored with motherhood, in fact bored with everything I valued. I'll never forget talking to her one day, trying to tell her what Montegiano meant to me. And I caught a certain look in her eyes—sheer blankness. She was just waiting for me to shut up.

'She wanted a grandiose apartment in Rome and a high-society life. That time I held out. We had our friends and I'd take her into Rome as much as possible, but I wouldn't move there permanently.

'When she realised I meant it, there was a bitter quarrel. That was when I discovered her real opinion of me, stuffy and dull, a man who couldn't give her the exciting life she wanted. She packed her bags, moved to the most expensive hotel in Rome and waited for me to crack. When I didn't, she returned after six weeks.

'I told myself she'd come back because she still loved me, but I believe she just liked the title, and still thought she could persuade me.

'It's been like that through the years. If she was thwarted she'd move out for a while and run up vast bills to punish me. I learned not to enquire too closely into what she got up to in the city.'

'You think she was unfaithful?'

'I'm sure of it.'

'Couldn't you have divorced her then? Or did you still love her too much?'

'No, the love died some time back, but I was reared in the tradition that said you don't break up the home, no matter what. And there was Renata. I had to think of what divorce would do to her. And now I've seen what it *has* done to her, I still think I was right.'

'What happened in the end?'

'Crystal started attending a gym in the city, said it was time to take proper care of her figure. Her instructor was

called Leo. I only saw him once, all greasy hair and gigolo smile.

'Suddenly she was pregnant. I even thought that perhaps we might have some hope after all, especially when
it was a boy. But then I heard her talking on the phone
to Leo, and it all became clear. I confronted her. She
called me every name she could think of, packed her bags
and left for good, with the baby, but without Renata.'

'Suppose she'd wanted Renata?' Joanna asked. 'Would
you have let her go?'

'Yes. I'd expect to have her back for long visits; after
all, she's my child too. But I'd let Renata do whatever
would make her happy.'

He leaned back and ran his hand through his hair, leaving it slightly ruffled. Joanna regarded him tenderly, and
reached for the phone to call Room Service. In a few
moments a waiter had arrived to remove the remains of
the meal. When the door had closed behind him Gustavo
moved to the large, comfortable sofa and sat down in a
way that was almost a collapse.

Joanna came over to an armchair near him, and poured
him a large whisky.

'Are you trying to get me drunk?' he asked with a grin.

'Possibly. I think it might do you good to let your hair
down for once. I won't tell on you.'

He took the tumbler and drained it. It pleased her to
see him more relaxed, although whether it was the
whisky or the relief of confiding in her, she couldn't tell.
But she found that she didn't care. It was sweet to reach
out to him and feel that she'd brought him some relief,
even perhaps a little contentment.

She found that he was smiling at her, a strange smile
that seemed to be sizing her up.

'Of course,' he said lightly, 'I blame you for everything.'

'Me? How?'

'Because it was entirely your fault that I married Crystal.'

CHAPTER SEVEN

'YOU were crazy for her,' Joanna reminded him.

'But I was engaged to you. If you'd held me to that we'd have married and lived happily ever after. Instead, you released me with quite indecent haste, abandoning me to my fate.'

'Oh, really?' she said, catching his ironic mood. 'So I should have been your nanny, should I?'

He sighed. 'Some men need nannies to stop them making fools of themselves. The melancholy truth is that I may be one of them.'

They laughed together.

'If I *had* held you to the engagement, would you really have married me?' she asked. 'You'd have let me coerce you?'

'You wouldn't have coerced me,' he said quietly. 'But you might have reminded me where my honour lay.'

'Love or honour,' she mused. 'It's an unequal contest. Anyway, where does honour lie?'

'That's the last question I expected you to ask.'

'You abandoned my large fortune for her small one because you really wanted to marry for love,' she pointed out. 'I call that honourable. I admired you for it. Truth to tell, I admired you for marrying Crystal more than for proposing to me. And if you'd let me force you into marriage, I'd have lost all respect for you.'

He was silent. What she was saying amazed him.

'But actually,' she went on, 'I don't think I could have held you to our engagement, whatever you think. I think

96

you'd have followed your heart anyway. At least, I hope you would.'

He stared at her. 'Do you mean that?'

'Of course I mean it. You put your love first, as a man should. It's not as though we were actually married. If we had been, and had children, that would have been different. You'd have had a duty to them. But you had none to me.'

He made a helpless gesture.

'I don't know how to answer that.' He thought for a moment. 'I never really knew you, did I?'

'No, not for a minute. Or I you. Gustavo, you're wrong about living happily ever after. We wouldn't have been happy together. You'd have been yearning for Crystal and resenting me for trapping you. Besides, do you think I have no pride? Who wants an unwilling husband?'

'And maybe you were secretly glad to be rid of me,' he mused.

She nodded. 'Maybe,' she said lightly.

He became awkward.

'Joanna, there's something I have to ask you. You may say that I have no right, and you'd be correct, but it's been puzzling—no, troubling me.'

'Go on.'

His voice was tense.

'Why did you agree to marry me in the first place?'

For one blinding moment Joanna was tempted to tell him the truth. After keeping the secret all these years, she had an overpowering need to reveal it, and surely she could risk telling him now?

But then she pulled herself back from the brink. He had come here for her help and she was about to pile more burdens onto him. For the knowledge of her love would be a burden if he could not return it.

So her shrug was a masterpiece of helplessness. 'Who knows? I believed in family expectations, just like you did. I was supposed to make a splendid marriage, and you were the best prize on the market. I was dazzled.'

'But by the time things fell apart you'd seen how little it all meant. You're right, our marriage wouldn't have worked. You needed something else, something that fulfilled and satisfied you more than I could ever do. You made a life that you chose for yourself, that was more important to you than any man.'

'Now you sound like Freddy. He used to accuse me of loving my ''other life'', as he called it, more than him.'

'Was it true?'

She nodded. 'I guess it was. Poor Freddy. It was good for a while, but I wasn't right for him. The only really good thing I did for him was to have Billy.'

'He's a son any parent could be proud of,' Gustavo reflected. 'A wonderful boy.'

'Yes, he is, isn't he?' she said, her face and voice softening as she thought of her darling.

'Is he very like his father?'

'In some ways. He gets his brains and his independence from me, and his outrageous charm from Freddy.'

'So your husband was very charming?'

'He *is*. He may not be my husband any more, but he'll be charming until the day he dies.'

Her smile as she said this made Gustavo observe, 'You sound as if you're still fond of him.'

'I am. Enormously. I've grown more and more fond of him since our divorce. He's kind, amusing and great fun. In fact, he's the perfect party guest, and great company as long as you're not actually married to him.'

'Why did you break up?'

'Well, he's not the most reliable man in the world.'

'Other women?'

Joanna laughed.

'He did his best to be faithful, but nature didn't make him that way. As I said, it's easier to be friends with him now that I'm not married to him, and his waywardness doesn't matter. The nicest thing I know about him is that he's a terrific father. Billy adores him, and with reason.

'Mind you, I think that's partly because Freddy's still a kid at heart. And he's such an impractical dreamer. He'd invent something, and I'd give him the funds to market it, but it always flopped. Then there'd be something else.'

'And you always funded him,' Gustavo said in a voice with a slight edge. 'I wonder if that had anything to do with— *No! No, I didn't say that. Please ignore it.*'

He dropped his head into his hands, appalled at himself. Joanna rocked with laughter.

'You mean he may have married me for my money,' she said at last. 'Surely people don't do that these days?'

'*Please, Joanna!*' His voice was muffled because his head was still sunk in an agony of embarrassment. 'Must you throw that up at me?'

'Throw what? Oh, *that*?' She clutched her head as though just remembering something. 'You mean because *you* were going to marry me for my money?'

He ground his teeth. 'If you choose to put it that way.'

'Oh, don't be so silly!' she chided him, smiling. 'That was completely different.'

'All right, laugh at me, but it *was* different. I really liked you a great deal. It would have been impossible otherwise.'

'I know, I know,' she said soothingly. 'I'm sorry, Gustavo, I didn't mean to make fun of you. Well, perhaps

I did, but only to cheer you up. You've got to admit it has its funny side.'

'Me, presuming to accuse your husband of mercenary intentions, you mean?'

'Not just that. Everything. The whole sorry mess. Oh, Gustavo, it wasn't meant to end like this. It wasn't what I...'

She had to stop and brush tears from her eyes. They had come suddenly, chasing away her laughter as she was swept by a sudden sense of futility.

'Wasn't what you what?' he asked. 'Joanna—'

'It's all right,' she said hastily. 'I only meant—it wasn't what I thought was going to happen.'

'I suppose what we expect never happens. Maybe there's no point in making plans at all.'

'You can't get through life without making plans,' she said wisely. 'You just have to be flexible about them.'

He passed a hand over his eyes. 'Perhaps I should have had a little less whisky. It's time I went to my own room. Before I go—what are you planning to do after this?'

'Well—'

'I ask because I'm invited to a wedding in a couple of days.'

'What wedding?' she asked with sudden suspicion.

'Lady Henrietta Rannley to Lord Askleigh. It's at Rannley Towers. I expect you'll be there too.'

'Well, she is my second cousin, once removed.' Her lips twitched. 'I suppose Billy's been talking again.'

'Billy was very helpful,' he said carefully, 'about more than the name of your hotel.'

She regarded him, telling herself that this was a time for straight, clear thinking. But it was hard to think at all, confronted by the discovery that he had fixed all this to be with her. In fact, it was impossible to do anything but feel happy.

I must have a word with Billy, she thought. And tell him, thank you.

'So it looks like we're both going,' she said. 'Imagine that! I'd planned to go tomorrow and stay the night at Rannley Towers, before the wedding. I'm beginning to think you're bound to have made the same arrangements, so why don't we go together?'

She'd avoided looking at Gustavo while she said this. Now, receiving no reply, she turned back to him and discovered the reason for his silence.

Gustavo lay back on the sofa, his head resting on the cushions, his eyes closed.

'Hey,' she said gently.

He didn't respond and she suddenly realised that he was deeply asleep. It had come on him suddenly, leaving him no choice but to yield. It would be unkind to awaken him.

Moving carefully, so as not to disturb him, she raised his feet until he was fully stretched out, then fetched a blanket from the bedroom and draped it over him.

She paused a moment to study his face, relaxed in sleep, yet still with the shadow of tension on it. With his guard down at last he seemed different, more like the very young man she remembered.

Was she only imagining that he looked like a man relieved of a crushing burden after many years?

She turned off the lamp near his head and dropped a kiss on his forehead.

'Goodnight,' she whispered. 'Sweet dreams.'

She went back to her room calling herself all kinds of a self-deceiver. When she'd thought of meeting Gustavo again she'd been so sure of herself, so convinced of her own strength and wisdom.

If he'd approached her with ardour, she could have coped. She still believed that. Instead he'd reached out to her in friendship and need, and by doing so he'd breached all her defences.

It was too late now. They had spoken not one word of love, and yet the feeling between them that night had been more intense than many lovers ever knew.

She would have laughed, years ago, to think that her love could come to this, but now it had happened and it was the sweetest, most joyous thing that had ever happened to her.

She wanted to shout her happiness aloud to the world. The way ahead was no clearer than it had ever been, but she had become his rock.

And if I have to be content with that, she thought, then I will.

But then—

The hell I will! I won't be content with second-best. This time I want it all.

In the morning she found the sofa empty. Gustavo appeared just as she was finishing breakfast.

'I was going to leave you a note to apologise for my boorish manners,' he said, 'but I couldn't think what to say. So I just crept out like a criminal and went to my own room.'

'Don't make so much of it.' She smiled. 'I'll be ready to leave in an hour.'

'I'll be waiting for you downstairs. And, Joanna— thank you for everything.'

He made no further reference to the evening they had

spent together, and the revealing things that had been said.

The train took them the fifty miles to the station near Rannley Towers, where they were met by Max, best man and brother of the groom. He'd never met Gustavo, but when he heard his name he looked startled and started to blurt out, 'Hey, aren't you the guy who…?' Then stopped and went red.

'Yes, that was me,' Gustavo said pleasantly. 'Shall we go?'

When they reached the house Etta came running to meet them. She too remembered Gustavo. As a child she'd been told little, but as a bridesmaid she'd worked out a good deal. Luckily she had more aplomb than Max, and the moment passed without trouble.

The huge house was rapidly filling up with guests staying the night. Many of them remembered Joanna and recognised Gustavo, but it was an old scandal, and after a few curious looks they forgot this odd couple, and concentrated on the bride.

Joanna had dreaded coming to this place for a wedding, fearful of the memories it would disturb. But suddenly everything was different. She was here with Gustavo, knowing that she was the person whose company he wanted. When everyone congregated for a meal that night she went down on his arm.

Passing through the hall, she caught a glimpse of the two of them in a long mirror and was struck afresh by his good looks, his upright bearing and a certain indefinable 'air' that would make any woman proud to be seen on his arm.

Her own appearance too had been transformed. She was no longer the gauche girl with no confidence in her own looks or personality. Now, in her soft blue gown, with diamonds in her ears and around her neck, she had the air of a woman who could take on the world and defeat it. Above all she looked as though she belonged with this handsome man.

As they walked, he turned slightly to glance at her. But for the mirror, she would never have noticed, but she saw the reflection of his quick look, the slight smile on his lips, the hint of pride in his eyes as he regarded her.

Then they moved on out of sight of the mirror. And when she next looked at him he was staring ahead, apparently oblivious.

It was a buffet meal so that the kitchen staff could concentrate on the demands of the wedding next day. This left the guests free to wander as they liked and Joanna's time was filled with renewing old friendships and catching up with her relatives.

Lord Rannley was particularly curious.

'What's going on?' he asked. 'You and him, here together?'

He was a charming man in his early fifties, with prematurely white hair that did nothing to mar his good looks. Joanna liked him, except that he was a little too eager to secure family advantage.

'Tommy,' she said now, 'if you're thinking what I'm thinking you're thinking, you can forget it.'

'So where's his wife? I heard rumours—'

'That's over. They're divorced.'

'And now he's here with you? Hmm!'

'I said forget it.'

'Really, my dear, you can't expect me to pass up the chance of adding a prince to the family. He slipped through our fingers last time but—'

'I'll tread on your toes in a minute.'

He grinned and dropped the subject, but a few moments later she saw him making friendly overtures to Gustavo. She could only hope that he wouldn't be too blatant about it.

She couldn't help noticing that, when Lord Rannley had left him, Gustavo wasn't at ease. The people here knew him only in connection with a past scandal, and he hated the feeling. But he'd wangled an invitation and braved the stares, simply to be with her.

'It's getting late,' she said to him at last. 'I'm going to bed.'

'Me too,' he said, as all around them guests were beginning to drift away.

They said their goodnights and went up the stairs together.

'It'll be a long day tomorrow,' she said.

'And perhaps a hard one.'

'We won't let it be,' she promised. 'Goodnight.'

She hugged him. He hugged her. And they went their separate ways.

In her new mood of contentment Joanna nodded off as soon as her head touched the pillow, and slept without a break until dawn.

But then she was unceremoniously awoken by someone plumping down on her bed. Hands shook her fiercely and an urgent voice said, 'Joanna, wake up, please. *Something absolutely terrible's happened.*'

'What? What's happened?'

Joanna struggled to awake and found Etta there, her face distraught.

'It's dreadful,' she wailed.

'What's dreadful? What's happened, Etta?'

'Gina's got flu,' she wailed.

'Hell!' Joanna said, not mincing matters. Gina was the matron of honour.

'Darling, could you do it for me, *please*? You're the same size and shape, and you'll fit into her dress.'

'Yes—yes—all right,' Joanna said, still half-asleep.

Etta gave her a resounding kiss. 'Bless you. Go back to sleep.'

She vanished, leaving Joanna to fall back on her pillows, eyes already closed.

She awoke again a couple of hours later, and immediately sat up in bed.

'Whatever did I say I'd do?' She dialled Etta's room on the bedside phone. 'Etta?'

'Yes, darling. Come right along and try your dress on. I've had your breakfast served here.'

Joanna hastily threw on her dressing gown and was in Etta's room a couple of minutes later.

'Did I imagine last night?'

'No, poor Gina's feverish. She's refusing all visitors until the wedding's safely over. Come and look at your dress.'

Joanna's eyes widened at the sight of that dress. Etta had had the idea of dressing her bridesmaids and her matron of honour in gowns identical to her own, save for slight variations of colour.

Etta's gown was satin-covered lace, cut on slender lines, with sleeves that trailed the floor. As befitted a bride, it was gleaming white.

The six bridesmaids all wore the same, but in pink, while Joanna's dress was also the same, in ivory. The only thing different was that the bride wore a long veil, while her attendants each had broad-brimmed hats of organdie, adorned with real flowers.

'It fits perfectly,' Etta said triumphantly when Joanna tried the dress on. 'You'll look wonderful. Now take it off so that we can have breakfast.'

In a daze Joanna ate some bread rolls and washed them down with coffee, listening to a stream of instructions, nodding and trying to concentrate.

'OK,' she said at last, donning her dressing gown. 'I'll dash back to my room for a shower, then I'll come straight back.'

She slipped back into the corridor, so preoccupied that at first she didn't see Gustavo. It was his sharp intake of breath that alerted her.

'Oh, good,' she said, laying a light hand on his arm.

To her astonishment he flinched.

'I was going to find you,' she said, 'to say that I won't be coming to the church in the same car as you after all.'

'I see.' His face was tense.

'The reason is—'

'There's no need for you to tell me the reason,' he said coldly. 'I should have realised.'

'Realised what?' she demanded, more and more puzzled by his strange tone and manner.

He didn't reply but his eyes roved over her dressing gown.

'You left it a little late to emerge,' he said. 'I believe discretion usually suggests an early-morning departure. People are so censorious.'

Suddenly his meaning dawned on her.

'Are you saying that you think—that *I*…? Gustavo, do you know whose room that is?'

'No,' he said, almost fiercely. 'Nor do I want to. You owe me no explanations.'

'I certainly don't. But you owe me an apology. How dare you think—what you are thinking? You ought to be ashamed of yourself.'

'Joanna…' he said uncertainly. Something in her blazing temper had got through to him.

'You really thought that I—?'

'I don't know what I was supposed to think.'

'Well, actually, you weren't supposed to think any-thing, because whose room you see me coming out of is none of your damned business. And that is especially true when you jump to insulting conclusions like some de-mented jack-in-the-box.'

'I did not mean to insult you—'

'Oh, really. Then would you like to give me a blow-by-blow account of exactly what you thought I was up to in there?'

'No, I wouldn't,' he said furiously, going slightly red.

'But you've got a really brilliant picture inside your head, haven't you? I doubt it bears any relation to the reality.'

'As you have said, it's none of my business. Now, if you don't mind—'

'But I do mind. You don't just make accusations and walk off—'

'I have not made any accusation—'

'Haven't you? Then what was that remark about early departures? Does that come from experience? How early are your departures, Gustavo?'

'I see no need to discuss it.'

'I'll bet you don't. But of course, if she has an apart-ment in Rome you don't need to leave early, do you? Or does she have nosy neighbours? Do you hide your face as you leave?'

'What the devil are you talking about?' he snapped.

'I'll tell you what I…'

But it was no use. She couldn't keep it up. Amusement was stronger than anger, and the next moment the laugh-ter welled up in her, bursting out so strongly that she had to clutch the wall.

'Joanna—'

'What an idiot you are!' she choked. 'But I suppose I'm an idiot as well. Just forget it.'

'Forget it? You make your opinion of me very clear and I'm supposed to forget it?'

'Well, you made your opinion of me very clear, but I forgive you.' Another gale of laughter swept over her. 'Oh, heavens, I shall die of this.'

His brow cleared a little at the implications of her amusement. His heart was beating as he had seldom felt it before. Not for twelve years, in fact.

He longed to ask her to tell him how wrong he was, but for the life of him he couldn't have got the words out.

Then, from behind the door, he heard a sound that seemed to restore him to life. A burst of female laughter. The next moment the door was flung open and Etta appeared. Over her shoulder he could see at least three other women in the room.

'Joanna, thank goodness you're still here. I'd like you to— Oh, hello.' She'd just seen Gustavo, and pulled the edges of her dressing gown together.

'Joanna's helping us out,' she explained. 'She's going to be my matron of honour instead of Gina, who has flu. Have you managed to explain to him yet, Jo?'

'I haven't had the chance,' Joanna said through quivering lips. 'Gustavo, I was going to find you and say there's been a change of plan. I'll be on duty with the bride.'

'Thank you for telling me,' he said stiffly.

Etta's eyes were like saucers as she looked from one to the other then made a tactful withdrawal.

Gustavo's face was tense and embarrassed, reminding Joanna of just how miserably uptight he could be, and how he, more than anyone, suffered for it. He was the last man in the world who could cope with this situation.

'How could you?' she said, amused and reproachful together.

'I apologise for—for—'

'Oh, shut up!' she said tenderly. 'I'll see you in the church.'

With one hand she touched his face while her lips just brushed against his other cheek. Then she slipped away without looking back.

CHAPTER EIGHT

THE wedding was held in the great church in the nearby town of Rannley Hayes. From ten o'clock a stream of cars began to leave the towers, and Joanna's sense of life playing back increased.

The last time she'd been to a wedding here she'd watched those same cars driving away, knowing that soon one of them would hold Crystal, glorious in bridal white, on her way to become Gustavo's wife.

She couldn't recall the weather then, but today the sun shone down with a glorious light as she got out of the car with Etta, helped to straighten her dress, then handed her the bouquet.

Then it was time to enter the church, where, since Etta's father was dead, Lord Rannley was waiting to give the bride away. The organ struck up the wedding march and they began the long walk down the aisle.

As matron of honour she led the attendants, walking down the aisle just behind the bride. Now and then she glanced to her right, trying to see where Gustavo was sitting, but there was no sign of him until the last minute.

There he was, near the front, in the second row, at the end of the pew, close to her. He turned as she approached, and Joanna was startled by what she saw in his face.

He looked stupefied, like a man who'd been struck by a thunderbolt, trying to gather his senses and failing.

She knew that for him too this moment brought back memories. Twelve years ago he'd stood in almost this

111

spot and watched his bride approach. Now his eyes were fixed on herself, and she thought she detected a question in them.

But she couldn't spare the time to wonder now what that question might mean. Etta had come to a halt, and she must take her bouquet of white roses, then step back into her position while the groom moved into place, and the service began.

'Dearly beloved, we are gathered here…'

Gustavo heard the words, the same ones that had been intoned over himself and Crystal. They seemed to come from a great distance.

He was only aware of Joanna, standing close to him, glorious in ivory satin and lace, her head adorned by the elegant organdie hat with its tiny pink rosebuds.

She looked like a bride herself, he thought. And so she would have been but for his blind stupidity. He'd been happy that day, but how soon that happiness had faded in the face of reality!

Was she too remembering, and wondering about how different things might have been?

He kept his eyes fixed on her, willing her to look at him, but she seemed lost in some inner dream. He longed to be able to follow her there, to beg her to share her thoughts with him, and perhaps also her feelings.

Too late. Much too late.

Dumbstruck by the terrible moment of illumination that had come to him, he listened to the vows of fidelity, remembering how they had come to sound like a cruel joke. As they would not have done with Joanna.

There was a lull as the bride and groom went into the vestry to sign the register, while the organist played a cheerful tune.

Joanna's head was in a whirl. Too much had happened

at once. She'd seen the funny side of this morning's incident, but she wondered now if she'd merely been trying to hide from reality. Gustavo had thought she'd spent the night with a man, and it had shattered him.

She wasn't looking at him, but she had no doubt that he was looking at her. Such was his control that she was sure his astonishment would no longer be reflected on his face. But it would still be there in his heart. She knew that, for it was the same with her.

Suddenly, high overhead, the organ pealed out in triumph. The newly married couple returned from the vestry to begin their journey back down the aisle and out into the sunshine.

Photographs. Dozens of them in various combinations. The happy couple with his family, with her family. Lord Rannley took charge of that one, contriving to draw Gustavo in so that he was standing just behind Joanna. As everyone crowded up together it was natural for him to put his hands on her shoulders.

It was only a light touch but Joanna found it unnerving. It made her think too intensely of all the ways she wanted him to touch her.

Then the pictures were over, and the new husband and wife got into their car together and drove back to the towers. Others cars were drawing up. The bridesmaids began to pile into a large limousine, and Joanna knew she must go with them.

She turned to give Gustavo a smile of goodbye, and as she did so a sudden gust of wind threatened to snatch off her hat. Before she could save it Gustavo had reached up quickly to settle his hands on the brim, and draw it down firmly on each side of her face.

'That's better,' he said, smiling into her eyes.

His hands lightly brushed her cheek, remaining there a moment, firm and gentle.

'Yes,' she said, breathlessly. 'That's better.'

She didn't see him again until they had returned to the towers and were finding their seats in the reception. As matron of honour she was on the top table. Gustavo was within sight but not next to her. She forced herself not to look at him. She couldn't trust herself to seem indifferent.

Speeches, toasts, all sounding much the same as before. Then the bride and groom took the floor and the dancing began.

Joanna did duty dances with the best man, the groom's brother and a series of men whose names she didn't know and didn't care about.

Then the happy couple departed on their honeymoon. Etta, full of mischief, tossed her bouquet in Joanna's direction, but Joanna was ready and stepped quickly aside.

'You made very sure to dodge that,' Gustavo said as they stood on the steps, waving the honeymooners off.

She hadn't realised that he'd noticed.

'Well, it's silly, isn't it?' she said lightly. 'It's just a quick way of making an idiot of yourself.'

'Is that a reference to Freddy?'

'Why should it be?'

'Because you caught Crystal's bouquet, I remember. It doesn't seem to have brought you much luck. Maybe you can't be blamed for being cautious now.'

She took his arm as they joined the others returning to the house.

'My marriage brought me Billy,' she said. 'I call that the best kind of luck. For the rest, there's a lot to be said for being footloose and fancy-free.'

As she spoke she gave him a challenging look that discomfited him.

'Is that aimed at me?' he asked, taking two tall glasses from a passing waiter and giving her one. 'I did apologise.'

'So you ought,' she said, teasing him over the rim with her eyes. 'Anyway, even if I had been…what you thought…well, it's a free country.'

'If you're trying to tell me that it's none of my business what you do—'

'Well, is it?'

'It might be,' he said, regarding her levelly.

She drank her champagne. It gave her time to collect her thoughts.

Outside, the light was fast fading. Inside the lights were coming on and refreshments were being served as the festivities started up again.

'It's been a strange day,' he said, drawing her over to the window, where they could have a little privacy.

'Yes,' she said, not pretending that she didn't understand his meaning.

'The wedding being in the same place—well, memories. Even poor Gina—'

'You mean me being matron of honour?'

'No, her getting flu and missing the wedding. That nearly happened to you. Remember how you got caught in the rain the night before, and we met in the corridor? You looked so wet and bedraggled I was worried about you.'

'Wet and bedraggled,' she mused. 'Yes, I was that all right. Inside and out.'

'What?'

'Nothing. I do remember, but I'm surprised that you do.'

'You didn't just pass out of my mind, Joanna.'

She gave a shaky laugh. 'Your memory's faulty. One look at Crystal and everyone passed out of your mind.'

'For a while. It was a madness, but it was soon over. And then there was nothing but the memories. Today was full of them.'

'Did they upset you?'

'No, I wasn't upset. That's all done with.'

'I hope it is.'

'Do you?' he asked quickly.

'It made you so unhappy, of course I'm glad it's over. There has to be some happiness waiting for you in the future, I'm sure of that.'

'Good,' he said quietly. 'If *you're* sure of it, well— let's talk later. The music's starting again. I've wanted to dance with you for hours. I've been patient, and waited my turn, but now I'm not going to be patient any longer.'

'But suppose I don't want to dance with you,' she teased, smiling.

He took her glass and set it down with his own, taking her into his arms.

'That can't be helped. You'll just have to put up with it.'

They were on the floor, spinning faster and faster so that she could barely get her breath. His arms about her were firm, drawing her close. The sedate, restrained young man she'd once known would never have held her like this, but this was another man, with a different agenda. Just what that agenda might be, she felt she was beginning to understand.

They might have been born to dance together, their bodies blending like fluid, anticipating each other's movements. She felt her excitement mounting, but it was an excitement of the heart as well as the body.

When the dance ended he didn't release her, but swept her straight into the next one.

'I can't breathe,' she laughed.

'Neither can I. Do you mind?'

'No—*no*!' She was giddy with joy, full of sweet sensations at the feel of his body pressed close to hers.

The music changed again, became a slow waltz. She watched his face, close to hers, and couldn't take her eyes from his lips, which were parted slightly. His warm breath touched her face.

'Joanna—'

'Yes…'

He began to move faster, dancing her towards an open door. As they went through it he kicked it closed. Then she was in his arms, drawn close while his lips sought hers, found them, covered them fiercely.

And in a moment all questions were answered. Everything in her yearned towards him. She had waited years for this moment, and she was going to relish it to the full.

In her mind she'd kissed him a thousand times but the reality was far sweeter. His lips were warm and firm on hers, urgent, demanding, and it was that demand that thrilled her most because everything in her longed to give to him. She would give him anything he asked—if only he would ask…

He cupped her face in his hands, looking into her eyes with an expression she wanted to see there forever.

But this was only a dream. She knew that because she'd dreamed it so often before. At any moment she would awaken, because nobody was allowed to be this happy. It would all be taken from her, but while it lasted she would revel in it.

'I think I've gone slightly mad,' he murmured.

'Yes, I think I have too, but I don't care. I don't mind being mad. I'm tired of being sensible.'

His smile was gentle. 'So am I. Joanna— Joanna—'

'Yes,' she whispered against his lips.

She closed her eyes as his mouth covered hers again and this time she let herself go completely, yielding to the joy of the moment as though nothing bad could ever happen again.

'Hello? Hello there? Is anyone here?'

She tried to blot out the man's voice but it reached her insistently.

'Hello!'

It was reality. It would not be denied.

'Anyone there?'

'Oh, no,' Joanna said despairingly.

'Let's get away before he sees us,' Gustavo whispered. 'It can't be us he wants.'

'But it is,' she groaned. 'Or at least me. That's Freddy, my ex, turning up like a bad penny.'

Gustavo cursed softly. Joanna wanted to rail against fate. It was too cruel that, at the moment when her heart yearned for Gustavo as fiercely as in the past, the miracle should be shattered so harshly. She was trembling, and she sensed the same in him.

'Hello!'

'It's no good,' she said. 'I'll have to talk to Freddy.'

'Tell him to go to hell.'

'I've tried that in the past. He just bounces back.'

Reluctantly they released each other and turned to see the man standing just inside the door. For the first time she realised that they were in semi-darkness.

'Hello, Freddy,' she said, trying to sound calm.

'Hello, Jo. Is that really you? I can't see you properly.'

She moved closer, and his face brightened.

'That's better. I say, you haven't got somebody with you, have you? Sorry to break it up and all that.'

'It's all right, Freddy,' she sighed. 'You haven't broken anything up. This is Prince Gustavo Montegiano.'

For the briefest possible moment Freddy seemed non-plussed.

'Uhuh!' in a noncommittal voice.

Then the moment was gone and he came closer, hand outstretched.

'Nice to meet you. You won't remember me, but I was at your wedding. Not exactly a gatecrasher, but brought along by a friend of a friend.'

'Whoever brought you, you were very welcome,' Gustavo said with slightly strained politeness. 'Did you, by any chance, reach this wedding in the same way?'

Freddy roared with laughter. 'Not this time. Mind you, I don't say I wouldn't have, if it had been necessary, but it wasn't. The groom's sister is a good friend of mine, if you know what I mean.'

He finished with a wink that made Joanna say in ex-asperation, 'Yes, we know what you mean, Freddy, and don't be vulgar.'

'I can't help being vulgar,' he said, hurt. 'I'm made that way. It's part of my charm.'

His face was broad, good-natured and as innocent as a baby's. It was the sort of face Gustavo guessed some women would find appealing. He would have liked to use his fists on it.

'I meant to be here sooner,' Freddy said, 'but I got a bit delayed. Sorry to break up the party and everything, but could I talk to you, please, Jo? It's really you I came to see.'

'Can't it wait until later, Freddy? Like tomorrow?'

His smile was beguiling. 'Ah, there's a problem about that. I'm only here for this evening, and there are things we need to discuss.'

'In that case, I'd better give in,' Joanna sighed.

Gustavo would have taken a wager that people usually gave in to Freddy because of what he described as his charm.

Whatever his charm was, Gustavo was sure he was immune to it.

Joanna shrugged at him helplessly. 'Sorry about this. I have to go.'

'To be sure. I must rejoin the party. Good evening, Mr Manton. It's been a pleasure meeting you.'

He walked out quickly.

He did as he'd said, returned to the party and spent the rest of the evening being the perfect guest. He smiled, he laughed, and all the time he wondered about Joanna. Had Freddy departed yet? And if not, what were they doing?

Then he saw them standing just inside the door, absorbed in conversation, or possibly in each other. Suddenly Freddy moved fast, sweeping her into the dance, twirling her around exuberantly. It was hard for him to make out her face as it flashed past, but Gustavo could tell that she was laughing as though she enjoyed his company.

After a while he made his excuses and went to bed.

As soon as he was alone with Joanna Freddy said, 'I can't see any sign of Billy.'

'No, he's not here. He was terrified he'd end up being a pageboy in satin—maybe even white satin.'

Freddy closed his eyes and winced in sympathy.

'So he kept well clear,' Joanna finished.

Freddy laughed. 'Wise man. Where is he, then? Not still in Italy on that dig he told me about?'

'Yes. I'm going back there tomorrow.'

'So when can I see him? I miss him like the devil, Jo.'

'Come and visit him at Montegiano. I'm sure Gustavo won't mind, and Billy will be thrilled.'

'Thanks,' he said, as eager as a boy himself. 'Now come and talk to me. We've got a lot of catching-up to do.'

She acquiesced, chiefly for Billy's sake. She would rather have been with Gustavo, but that was ruined for the moment. Once broken, the spell could not be recaptured tonight. But there would be another time, she promised herself. And soon.

In the meantime, she made the best of it and found, yet again, that, if you weren't married to him, Freddy was great company. They spent a couple of happy hours discussing Billy, and finished the evening on the dance floor.

'What time do you have to go?' she asked as the lights began to fade, and the band packed up.

'Go?' Freddy asked innocently.

'You said you were only here for a few hours.'

'Ah, yes, so I did.'

'I see,' she said with a resigned sigh.

'I only came on the off-chance because I heard you were going to be here at the last minute. I thought Billy might be with you, or, at any rate, that we could have a good talk. Which we did.'

'But why didn't you just call me and ask about Billy?'

'Ah, well…' He became mysteriously awkward. 'There was another reason but—let's leave that for the moment.'

'All right. Do you have somewhere to sleep?'

'Yes, they're letting me have the groom's bed, since he's gone now.'

'Fine, then I'll see you in the morning.'

She kissed his cheek and went in search of Gustavo. But there was no sign of him, and someone told her that he'd gone to bed.

On the day after the wedding Gustavo was down early, hoping to catch Joanna alone. There was no sign of her in the breakfast room, where a buffet meal was laid out, so he poured himself a coffee and went to look out of the window.

The next moment he drew back out of sight. In the distance he'd seen Joanna and Freddy wandering beneath the trees, deep in conversation. It was too far for him to tell what they were saying, but their heads were close and they seemed at ease with one another.

Gustavo risked one more look and saw that they were heading towards the house. He went to the table where the food was laid out and tried to help himself to something, but all he could hear was the echo of Freddy saying, 'I'm only here for this evening.'

Something had happened to change his mind. Had that anything to do with Joanna's welcome, which had obviously become warmer when they were alone?

They were nearer now, enough for him to hear Freddy saying, 'I can't help it if I've got a magnetic appeal.'

And Joanna's reply, 'Yes, and you live on it.'

'I have to. It's all I've got.'

'Oh, no, it isn't. I gave you a very good settlement.'

'True, but actually, I was hoping to—'

'How much?' Joanna sounded both amused and resigned.

'I've got this opportunity for a little investment—'

'I know your little investments. I should by this time. Oh, all right. Put down the details and I'll call the bank.'

'You're a darling. And you still find me appealing, don't you? You laugh at my jokes, anyway.'

'You make good jokes, I've never denied that.'

'You see, you still care for me.'

'I've never denied that either. You're great fun, Freddy, but I wouldn't be married to you again for all the tea in China.'

'You wouldn't get the chance. I've replaced you several times over.'

'You didn't wait for the divorce to do that,' Joanna said wryly.

There was a brief silence before Freddy said, 'And may I remind you, my darling, that there's more than one way to be unfaithful? Oh, forget it. We agreed, no hard feelings on either side.'

'Yes,' she said, and Gustavo wondered if he only imagined the note of relief in her voice.

He was ashamed of himself for eavesdropping, but once he'd started to listen nothing could have made him draw back. For some reason he needed to know what sort of relationship Joanna had with the man whose wife she'd once been. What he heard left him not knowing what to think.

But he would have given a good deal to know how to interpret 'there's more than one way to be unfaithful'.

A moment later there was a step outside the room, and Gustavo turned to see Freddy enter alone.

'Coffee?' he asked politely.

'Thanks,' Freddy said. 'Well, well, fancy it being you!'

'You mean you've heard that old story? Well, it's history now, and there's no more mileage to be had out of it,' Gustavo said, keeping his voice light.

'Anything you say.' Freddy accepted the coffee and spooned in a generous amount of sugar. Seeing Gustavo regarding him he said, 'I've got a very sweet tooth.'

'So I would have imagined.'

Freddy gave a slight frown. He wasn't normally quick on the uptake but there was no mistaking Gustavo's tone.

'Meaning?' he asked. 'Meaning?'

'Let's just say that Joanna is a very generous woman.'

'Oh, you heard that last bit? Well, yes, she is a generous woman, but I'm a very tolerant man. It's not easy for a man when she's so much richer than he is. There's always that inequality, and you can't help feeling it. But I did my best to cope.'

Gustavo turned away to conceal his disgust. But in the next moment a picture flashed into his mind.

Joanna's suite at the Ritz, the most expensive the hotel had to offer. And his own single room, so much cheaper.

There's always that inequality, and you can't help feeling it.

Who was he to censure this man for seeking Joanna's money?

He recalled the indulgent half-contempt in her voice as she'd yielded to Freddy's pleas. She was used to men who were after her money. They were probably the only kind she'd ever known. Starting with himself.

And, like the voice of the serpent, there came into his ear the sound of Joanna saying, 'You abandoned my large fortune for her small one. I call that honourable.'

'Hey, are you all right?' Freddy clapped a hand on his shoulder.

'Yes,' Gustavo said, with difficulty. 'Yes, I'm all right.'

He got out fast before he did something violent.

On the way up to his room he met Joanna coming down. She smiled and touched his arm.

'I'm sorry to dash off and leave you last night, but I really had to talk to Freddy.'

'Obviously there was a lot to talk about,' he said, trying to keep an edge out of his voice, and not quite succeeding.

'It was mostly about Billy. He isn't seeing as much of him as he'd like, so we had to work something out.'

'And it took all night? He was supposed to be leaving yesterday.'

She smiled wryly. 'He only said that to get my attention. I'm afraid Freddy tends to say whatever is convenient at the moment. That's the kind of man he is.'

'Astonishing!'

'What does that mean?'

'Nothing, I'm just in a bad mood.'

'Gustavo, I have a confession to make. Freddy wants to see Billy. He has every right and Billy loves to be with him, so—'

He groaned. 'So he's coming to stay with us? When?'

'I don't know. Do you mind?'

'Would it make any difference if I did?'

Laughing ruefully, she shook her head.

'Hello there!'

The shout behind them made them turn and groan simultaneously.

'What's up, Freddy?' Joanna said.

'Well, I thought it was time we were on our way to Italy.'

'We?' Gustavo echoed ominously.

'Yes, didn't Jo say she'd invited me?'

'She has just informed me of the honour of your visit,' Gustavo said glacially.

'Honour? That's very kind of you but there's no need to go overboard. A bed in the corner will do me.'

'I think we can manage a little better than that,' Gustavo said with terrifying courtesy. 'So, we three shall travel to Rome together.'

'Jolly good!' Freddy whipped out his cellphone. 'I'll let Billy know now.'

'No, don't.' Joanna put a hand on his arm. 'Surprise him. Think of his face when you walk in.'

Freddy beamed. 'What a sight!'

'I'll call and book the tickets,' Joanna said.

'Be sure to let me know how much I owe you,' Gustavo said firmly.

'Get first class,' Freddy called. 'More leg room.'

'You'll fit yourself into whatever I can get,' she called back cheerfully.

Left alone, the two men eyed each other. Gustavo's dislike was mixed with unease, but he doubted if anything in the world could make Freddy uneasy, unless it was a bill and no Joanna to pay it.

CHAPTER NINE

JOANNA managed to get three first-class tickets to Rome, landing at seven o'clock that evening.

'I called Billy and said I'd be there tonight,' she told Gustavo as they flew over France later that day.

'Did you weaken after all, and tell him his father's coming?'

'No, I don't want to spoil the surprise. But he'll be thrilled. They're just kids together. My only fear is that Billy's growing up so fast that he's soon going to find his father a little young for him. But he's so kind-hearted that I expect he'll hide that.'

'Freddy's a lucky man. Tell me something—has Billy ever blamed you for Freddy's disappearance?'

'You mean in the way Renata blames you? No. But then Freddy hasn't actually disappeared. They're in touch all the time, either talking or texting.'

Gustavo sighed. 'Yes, that's it, isn't it?'

'Do you hear from Crystal?'

'I believe she's in Paris right now, with her gigolo. She's sent Renata some postcards, mostly talking about the wonderful time she's having.'

She squeezed his hand sympathetically, and he squeezed in return. But she knew it wasn't the moment to try to draw him back to the mood that had been shattered last night, especially with Freddy sitting just across the gangway.

At Rome they went through the formalities of entry. As they came out of Customs Joanna, who was walking first, saw Carlo with Billy. She made frantic signs for the boy to look behind her, then stepped aside, giving him a good view of Freddy. The next moment the child's shriek and the man's yell split the air.

'*Dad!*'

'*Billy!*'

Then they were in each other's arms, hugging tightly, swinging around and around, while people passing by stopped to stare and smile at such happiness.

Laughing with pleasure, Joanna turned to see Gustavo, also watching them, and the look on his face broke her heart. There was no child here to greet him.

'Renata's in bed,' Carlo said quickly. 'She didn't sleep well last night, so Laura thought—you know—'

'Of course,' Gustavo said in a toneless voice. 'I'm sure Laura knows best.'

Getting everyone into the car was a tight squeeze.

'I didn't know there was going to be a third person,' Carlo explained apologetically.

'No matter,' Gustavo said. 'You all go ahead, I'll get a taxi.'

'I'll come with you,' Joanna said.

'No, go with your son.'

'Are you kidding? He's got his father; he doesn't need me right now.'

But Billy called to her, 'Come on, Mum. Come in here with Dad and me.'

'Go on,' Gustavo said quietly and walked away without waiting for an answer.

Billy came and grabbed her by the hand, pulling her to the car. 'It's gonna be great, all being together,' he said.

'Of course it is, darling,' she said cheerfully, not wanting to spoil it for him.

But inwardly her heart ached for Gustavo, returning to his home alone because there was nobody there who wanted him.

At the *palazzo* Joanna was greeted by the housekeeper with the news that her new room was ready.

'My new room?' she queried.

'His Excellency telephoned me with instructions that Signor Manton was to be put in the Julius Caesar room and move you to a suite on the next corridor.'

'I thought it would be nice for him to be next to Billy,' Gustavo said when she went to find him. 'I was sure you'd feel the same, since you are so anxious for them to enjoy each other's company. I don't think you'll have any complaints about your new accommodation.'

It was certainly magnificent, and it seemed as though nothing could be more genial than Gustavo's concern for his new guest, although she suspected him of a hidden agenda.

Freddy, popping along to see her, whistled at the sight, and immediately pinpointed her suspicion.

'He's taken care to put you a long way away from me, hasn't he?'

'Nonsense. He was thinking of you.'

'Sure, and I'm very glad to be next to Billy. But why did he move you as far away as this?'

'Freddy, I'll get cross with you in a minute.'

'That's right, darling, you do that. I always knew when I'd hit the nail on the head, because it made you so mad.'

He laughed and went off to find Billy, leaving Joanna wishing she knew what to think.

Almost at once she was plunged back into work. The team descended on her, eager to bring her up-to-date, and for days she hardly left the dig.

She felt as if she was floating in limbo. She had shared

with Gustavo a moment of incredible sweetness, spoiled by Freddy's untimely arrival. Now she longed to reach out and catch once more at the whispering shadows of that moment, perhaps even reclaim it entirely. But somehow the time was never right. Freddy's presence in the house was an inhibition, and Gustavo himself seemed content to let things remain like this, not going out of his way to be with her. Sometimes she almost wondered if she had imagined everything.

But then she would look up and catch an unguarded expression in his eyes. She hadn't imagined anything. What she'd sensed that night was still there, but he was trying to deny it.

He seemed to have withdrawn, not just from herself, but from everyone. He no longer tried to reach out to Renata, as though finally accepting her rejection and unwilling to risk a further snub.

To make matters worse Renata had an instant rapport with Freddy. He and Billy had quickly admitted her as a third to their mutual-adoration society and she knew no greater joy than to help Billy show his father around.

Freddy even knew enough basic Italian to get by with his son's help. Although academically useless he had a good ear and could muddle his way through a conversation, making up anything he didn't know, and reducing both children to giggles.

Sometimes the three of them came out to the dig. Renata had warmed to Joanna, evidently feeling that Billy's mother must be all right. She was there on the day Hal discovered an unusual decorative tile that caused everyone to become excited.

'This pinpoints it,' Joanna said. 'They used this style of decoration at the start of the fifth century, which means—'

She wasn't sure how much the children understood, but they joined in the cheers. In the middle of the commotion Joanna looked up to see Gustavo standing there, watching, isolated, and her heart ached for him.

That night he was missing from the evening meal, but as Joanna was about to go upstairs he opened his study door and beckoned her in.

'Do you remember Pietro and Maria Faloni?'

'Yes, they came to dinner when I was here before. They were—very elegant.'

She couldn't have spoken of them more warmly than that. They had been a newly married couple, pleasant company, but rather too socially conscious to appeal to Joanna. She was sure Maria thought her dowdy.

'They want to give a party in your honour,' Gustavo said.

'Really? My stock must have risen in the world.'

'You're a celebrity. I warn you Maria collects celebrities and she'll give me no peace until I take you.'

'I'll need some new clothes. I take it this will be formal.'

'Extremely. White tie and tails.'

Her eyes twinkled. 'I don't look good in white tie and tails.'

He had to think for a moment. 'Oh, yes, I see.'

'It was a joke,' she told him sadly.

'Of course. I'm sorry. I guess Crystal was right.'

'About what?'

'She always said I was too stuffy for any woman to put up with.'

'She didn't know what she was talking about,' Joanna said angrily.

'Maybe. I'm afraid my capacity for jokes has rather left me these days.'

'Don't take any notice of Crystal. Much she knows! Now let's forget her. I want to dress up and have fun.'

It felt good to be going to a glamorous party again, to have an excuse to buy a couture dress that made the best of her height, tiny waist and long legs.

Poor Aunt Lilian, she thought. You said most girls would give their eye-teeth to be my size, and I was so ungrateful. I'm not ungrateful any more.

The dress was black silk, narrow in the waist and low in the front, revealing a bosom that was more generous since Billy's birth. The side was slashed to just above the knee.

There was just time to have her hair cut and styled the way she wanted it. With dainty silver sandals on her feet and diamonds in her ears her appearance was complete. She returned to the estate with a pile of boxes, feeling like a pirate who'd just come back from a raid, and hid her booty in her room.

True to his word, Gustavo appeared in white tie and tails and she was taken aback by how well they suited him. With his height and breadth of shoulder, he might have been born for formal clothes.

He waited for her in the study and she entered casually, refusing to let him see she was eager for his reaction.

When it came it lived up to all her hopes. He said nothing, simply looking at her in silence for a long time. Then smiling.

'Will I do?' she asked lightly.

He nodded, and she sensed him struggling for words. 'You'll do.'

Detecting a shadow in his manner, she asked, 'Is anything wrong?'

'No,' he said a little too quickly. 'Let's go.'

She didn't press the point, but she noticed that he hastily locked a paper away in his desk drawer before turning back to her with a smile.

The chauffeured limousine was waiting outside. Gustavo offered her his arm and they went out together. Throughout the journey he sat turned towards her, his eyes resting on her. He didn't speak, but he didn't need to.

The Falonis lived in a palatial apartment on the Via Veneto. When the limousine had dropped them they went up three floors in the elevator to be received eagerly by Pietro and Maria.

Maria clasped Joanna in her arms then stepped back to take in her whole appearance, and give a little nod of satisfaction.

'I wouldn't have known you,' she said.

'Thank you,' Joanna said.

They understood each other.

'I am so excited,' Maria confided as she ushered Joanna inside. 'Everyone's been dying to entertain you, but I swore I'd get you first.'

'Really? Why?'

'Don't be modest, my dear. You're *the* catch of the season. Everyone's talking about you and that discovery, but you hide yourself away like a mystery woman. My friends are going to be *so* annoyed that I got you first.'

Joanna enjoyed Maria's company more now than before. She was so blatant in her snobbery that it became amusing, and she showed off her guest of honour with a pride that gave a fillip to Joanna's ego, resist it how she might.

The Falonis lived at the top of Roman society, and the people Maria could gather was staggering. There were two government ministers and a film star, causing Joanna to doubt that she could really be the guest of honour. But this was Italy, a country with a vibrant interest in its own past. Everyone had met the other celebrities before.

There was even a well-connected journalist who wrote a waspish gossip column for the society pages. When he simpered and asked Joanna if the Montegiano site was really the find of the century, everyone held their breath.

But Joanna was equal to the challenge.

'Considering that this century is only a few years old, I think I can say definitely yes. If you'd asked me about the last century I'd have to be more cautious.'

Everybody laughed and there was a smattering of applause for the adroit way she'd avoided the trap. Even the man who'd tried to bait her raised his glass in salute, and a few minutes later he engaged her in a serious discussion that was at variance with his former manner.

The others began to crowd around, and soon she realised that she was practically giving a lecture.

Gustavo tried to stay in the background. He had a strange feeling of watching Joanna at a distance. The perspective seemed to change every moment, both confusing and delighting him.

He'd seen her in shabby old clothes, bustling around the dig, giving orders to her team, laughing with them but always very much the boss.

In England she'd been the comforting friend, offering her arms to hold him and her gentle wisdom to help him. Then he'd seen her as a bride again, and moved closer to an unknown land that he now realised had been haunting him for years. It was still there, tantalisingly just out of reach.

But watching her now, at ease in these surroundings, dominating the crowd with her beauty, wit and expertise, he saw a new Joanna. Marrying her would be like marrying at least four women.

He tried to shut his thoughts off there, but they persisted in straying into forbidden territory.

With sudden decisiveness he rose from his chair and went over to her. The 'lecture' was over and she was flirting with three men at once.

'If you're tired we could go home,' he suggested.

There was a roar of disapproval and cries of 'Spoilsport'. Joanna looked at him, her eyes glinting with fun.

'Am I tired?' she teased.

He laid his hand persuasively on her arm.

'I think you might be,' he said softly.

'In that case—'

She stopped because a man behind her had given a sharp intake of breath. Gustavo too had seen something that filled him with dismay. Turning her head, Joanna saw Crystal standing in the doorway, as beautiful as the fairy on the tree.

In that frozen moment only one thought pervaded Joanna's mind.

Dammit! She *would* have to be wearing black too!

It was ludicrous, but for a moment it would serve as a shield between herself and the full wretchedness of the situation.

Like Joanna, Crystal had gained from the years. She was as dainty as ever, her hair as perfectly blonde, but experience had added a knowingness to her face.

It was true that, like Joanna, she wore black, but there the similarity stopped. Her dress was very tight and very short, revealing a pair of stunning legs.

For a long moment she stood still in the doorway, allowing her effect to sink in. Then she smiled and came forward to Maria, arms outstretched.

'Dear Maria, I'm positively in sackcloth and ashes. It's dreadful of me to gatecrash your party, isn't it?'

Since the only possible response to this was a denial, Maria obliged, embracing Crystal with apparent warmth, although her eyes flickered nervously to Gustavo and Joanna. But both had recovered themselves sufficiently to appear untroubled.

Crystal turned her big guns on to Joanna.

'Jo, *darling*, how lovely to see you after all this time. And so famous now! I'm really honoured to be allowed into your presence.'

She enveloped her in an embrace, which gave Joanna the chance to mutter in her ear, 'Don't be an idiot, Crystal. It's a good act but you're overdoing it. Actually, you always did.'

Crystal drew back just enough to smile into her face and murmur, 'I know, darling, but when time is short, overdoing it can be very useful.'

She surveyed Joanna fully.

'My, you have improved! Everything they say about you is true.'

Not for the world would Joanna have asked what 'they' said about her. She merely raised her eyebrows satirically and replied, 'Is that so? I doubt if the same could be said about you.'

She saw with satisfaction that Crystal wasn't sure how to take this. She turned away and began working the room, managing to draw the ministers and film star into her web at the same time, not seeming to notice Gustavo, whose face was very pale.

The party, which had briefly paused, began to swirl around them again. Joanna saw Gustavo turn away and take a few deep breaths. The sight dismayed her. Perhaps she'd been wrong about everything if Crystal could still affect him like this.

He came to her side.

'What the devil is she doing here?' he muttered. 'She's supposed to be in Paris.'

'You didn't have any warning of this?'

'Good God, no!' he said violently. 'Do you think I'd have brought you here if I'd known?'

'Shall we leave?'

'I think that would be a good idea. Let's find our hostess.'

But the next moment Crystal laid a hand on his arm.

'Gustavo, my dear, you surely aren't avoiding me, are you?'

'I was being tactful, Crystal. People are watching us with interest.'

'I know. Isn't it fun?'

'I don't find it fun to be stared at.'

'No, you never did know how to enjoy yourself.'

'Our ideas about enjoyment were always different,' he growled.

'Darling, our ideas about everything were different. Let's not go over that old ground again. The thing is that I do need to talk to you privately. Joanna won't mind, I know. Let's go out onto the balcony.'

Gustavo turned to Joanna, stiff with awkwardness at the scene Crystal had forced on him.

'If you'll excuse me for a moment.'

'Of course,' she said, sounding as cheerful as possible, trying to make him feel easier. 'You two go and talk.'

'And you go back to your admirers,' Crystal said, making Joanna wonder just how long she'd been there. 'My, what a success you've had! Tomorrow, all Rome will be talking about you even more than they already are.'

She went straight out of the glass door leading to the balcony.

'Go on,' Joanna urged him. 'Of course you two need to talk. I'll be fine.'

'With your admirers?' he echoed edgily.

'Of course. The more the better. Go and talk to her.'

But he stood looking at her, an unaccustomed fierceness in his eyes. A rush of something—jealousy? cunning?—made her say, 'If you can cosy up to Crystal I can cosy up to whoever I please.'

'I am not cosying up to her and you know it,' he said furiously.

'Better ask what her plans are.'

He ground his teeth. 'You're the one who's urging me to follow her out there.'

'Yes, so go.'

'Joanna—'

'*Go!*'

Glowering, he went out onto the balcony. Joanna watched him leave, wondering what had come over her. It had been a stupid, irrational spat that made no sense at all.

And she felt a thousand times better for it.

One of her flirts approached her, offering champagne.

'No, thank you,' she said kindly. 'What I'd really like is a nice cup of tea.'

Outside, in the cool air of the balcony, Gustavo stood regarding Crystal.

'I thought you were in Paris,' he said. 'That was your last excuse for not coming to see your daughter.'

'I got home from Paris last week. How is poor little Renata?'

'Very unhappy. And she wouldn't be "poor little Renata" if you gave her some of your attention. When are you coming to see her?'

'When I can. I've so much to see to just now. I'm

buying an apartment in Rome and it's taking up all my time.'

'Well, at least if you're living in Rome you'll be able to see Renata a good deal.'

'I wish you wouldn't keep harping on about that,' Crystal said fretfully. 'It's much better for her to be with you. My life wouldn't suit her at all.'

'I'm not talking about her living with you, but visiting you, once you're living in Rome. She'll be able to visit you a lot now, *won't she*?'

'Well, I expect we'll sort something out,' Crystal said vaguely. 'But that's not what I brought you out here to talk about. Have you had a letter from my lawyer yet?'

'Yes, it came this morning.'

'Well?'

'What do you expect me to say, Crystal? You know I can't find a sum like that at a moment's notice.'

'Hardly a moment's notice. It's months since I left. You've had plenty of warning.'

'Yes, but our agreement was that the rest of what I owed you could be paid next year.'

'I know, I know, but I need it now. Things have changed. I want to get on with my life.'

'Where's your boyfriend? He doesn't seem to be here tonight.'

'Oh, him,' she said dismissively. 'That's all over.'

'So soon?'

She shrugged. 'He was all right for a while. He had certain—talents.'

'Yes, you mentioned that at the time,' he said coldly. 'I gather his talents weren't enough in the long run.'

'I got bored with him,' she admitted. 'He wanted us to settle permanently in Naples and have lots and lots of *bambini*.'

'No, I remember that lots and lots of *bambini* never did fit into your schedule, did they?' Gustavo said drily.

'Well, anyway, we're not together now,' Crystal said, adroitly sliding away from the subject. 'There was no way I was going to bury myself in Naples, *bambini* or no *bambini*. So I left him.'

'Despite his remarkable talents?'

She shrugged. 'There are other talented men in the world. I'm ready to start again, and I want the rest of my money.'

'Crystal, for pity's sake, I'm doing my best, but I can't produce it just like that. Surely you can be patient a little longer?'

'It seems that I'm going to have to be. Just don't make me wait too long. After all, you've got that huge estate. You can borrow against it.'

'Have you any idea how much I had to borrow to pay you the first half of the money? Of course not.'

'How could I? In any case, I've never understood much about money unless it was in large, simple amounts.'

'Well, we're talking about a large, simple amount now, and it's more than I can raise so quickly.'

'Oh, really, darling, don't be silly. Of course you can raise it. There's always Joanna.'

His face tightened. 'And what exactly do you mean by that?'

'She's worth far more than I ever was. People say you and she are as thick as thieves these days. So it's easy. All you have to do is marry her.'

CHAPTER TEN

GUSTAVO stared as though he couldn't believe what he had heard.

'What—did you say?' he asked slowly.

'I said you should marry Joanna. Really, darling, don't be dense. She's got enough money to solve all your problems.'

When he still didn't speak she came closer.

'And then you could afford anything you wanted—including getting rid of me. Isn't that a tempting prospect?'

'That's enough!'

There was genuine rage in Gustavo's voice, enough to silence her, if only for a moment.

'Don't ever speak like that again,' he snapped. 'Don't even think it at the bottom of your scheming little mind.'

'All right, all right, there's no need to be like that. I'm only thinking of your welfare.'

'You were thinking of what suited you, and nothing else.'

'Well, I don't know what you're making such a fuss about. You need a rich wife and there aren't many who are richer than her. Goodness knows what she's doing working for a living.'

'Yes, you wouldn't understand that, would you?' he said harshly. 'Joanna works because she loves her subject more than anything in the world, except her son.'

'More than you?'

The question attacked him like a knife, making him draw in a sharp breath.

At last he spoke emphatically. 'Joanna does not love me.'

She surveyed him, her head on one side.

'Really? Well, I dare say you'd know all about that. Besides, there's no need to despair. With a little effort I'm sure you could make her love you—'

'Drop it,' he said in a low voice. 'Drop it if you know what's good for you.'

Crystal sighed. 'Oh, darling, how touchy you are. She's your best chance, and you'd be wise to take it and then—'

She checked herself and backed off at the murderous look in Gustavo's eyes.

'Go to hell!' he told her with soft fury. 'Go to hell and stay there. *Do you understand me?*'

On the last words he raised his voice enough for it to carry faintly beyond the glass doors into the room, so that those standing nearest jumped and turned their heads. The next moment Gustavo erupted through the door and went straight to Joanna.

'If you're ready—' he said.

'Of course,' she said, wondering what could have happened to make him so pale.

He got through the farewells to their hosts as quickly as he could square with courtesy before drawing her out of the room. The last thing Joanna saw was Crystal, looking like the cat that had swallowed the cream. It was a look she recalled from long ago, and it made her shiver.

Not until they were shut into the back of the limousine and the chauffeur was starting the engine did Joanna say, 'For heaven's sake, what happened? Why were you shouting?'

'Because that woman…' He clenched his hands, real-ising the impossibility of telling Joanna anything about that conversation. 'I can't talk to her without getting angry.'

'Do you think she went there on purpose?'

'Oh, yes, she knew we were going to be there.'

'What about the fitness instructor?'

'She left him in Naples. Apparently it's all over.'

A tremor went along her nerves. She tried not to heed it.

'So she's back for good?' she asked lightly.

'She now has an apartment in Rome, and is talking about getting on with her life.'

'Was that what she wanted to tell you, and that made you so angry?'

'No, it was something else. Don't ask me, I can't tell you.'

His tone was abrupt because he felt hideously embar-rassed by Crystal's words. He resented the way she'd intruded on the delicate feelings that had been growing between himself and Joanna recently.

It was something he'd never known before, totally dif-ferent from his passion for Crystal, which had blazed across the sky like a comet before dying abruptly. He knew now that his love for her had been almost entirely physical, taking no account of the person she was. And when he'd discovered that person, the love was over.

With Joanna it was the reverse. He treasured her warmth, her gentleness and understanding, the mysterious sense that she held the world in her hands and could share it with him. Desiring her had come later.

She was the woman he wanted. Twelve years ago it had been too soon. Now the time was right for them.

Or, at least, for him. About her he was still unsure. To

Crystal he'd given an instinctive denial, appalled by the way her cynicism was dirtying something so precious. But secretly he was still waiting to learn the truth.

Joanna had fallen silent and he realised that his tone must have sounded like a snub.

'Forgive me,' he said gently. 'I shouldn't take it out on you. I don't know what I'm saying. I just wish I could turn the clock back to before tonight.'

She gave a faint smile that he could only just make out in the gloom of the car.

'No use,' she murmured. 'I've often wanted to turn the clock back.'

'Yes, so have I. But I can never quite decide how far back to go.'

'To the last moment of happiness?' she said. 'Or the last moment before a terrible mistake? Or perhaps it doesn't matter, and we'd make the same mistake again. Because you couldn't look into the future and see what was waiting, any more than you could the first time.'

'Joanna, you're talking mysteries. What mistakes could you ever have made?'

She shook her head ruefully. 'Don't take any notice of me, Gustavo. I'm talking nonsense.'

He leaned closer, trying to see her face, wanting to know if the half-smile he fancied he saw was real, and, if so, what it meant.

'You never talk nonsense,' he said. 'It always means something, and it's always something that I want to know about.'

She shook her head. 'Now it's I who cannot tell you. You must let me have my secrets.'

But he too shook his head. 'No, I want to know your secrets. Every one of them. I want to know what you're thinking and feeling. I want—I want *you*.'

He had sworn not to say it, but he was no longer in command of himself. He knew that he should not take her into his arms and kiss her, but nothing could have stopped him.

He knew now that he'd meant this to happen since the night of the wedding, the night that had been interrupted. Since then, whatever he'd been doing, at any moment of the night or day, he'd been thinking of her, needing her, wanting her.

To Joanna it was a thousand kisses in one. It was here and now, but it was also every kiss he'd ever given her in her dreams. But then she dismissed the dreams: ghostly memories, yearning fantasies. They had no reality against the man, warm and solid in her arms, covering her mouth with purposeful lips.

Her own lips moved against his, seeking him more deeply, thrilling as he responded with an urgency that was a promise.

A flash of light from a car coming in the other direction recalled them to their surroundings, and the presence of the chauffeur.

'We'll be home soon,' Gustavo said in a slightly strained voice.

'Yes,' she murmured, settling herself in the crook of his arm, her head against his shoulder.

For now this was all she asked, to be here with him in peace and tranquillity. Soon she would want much more from him, but it was what he wanted too, and that knowledge was part of the joy now.

So deep was her contentment that she almost dozed, until she heard him say, 'We're here,' just over her head.

They got quietly out of the car, trying to keep their arrival a secret from the rest of the house. Inside, he didn't switch on any lights, but stood looking at her face in the faint glow from the hall lamp. There was a question in his eyes, which she answered by laying her lips on his for a brief moment.

'Come,' she said, taking his hand and leading him up the stairs.

Nobody saw them as they passed quietly down the corridor to her room and closed the door behind them.

'Don't put the light on,' he whispered. 'We don't need light.'

'No,' she said. 'We don't need anything but this.'

She stepped back and removed the gold from her ears.

'Turn around,' he said, and began to work at the clasp of her gold necklace. She felt the touch of his fingers, setting off soft tremors of desire that whispered across her heated skin. When he'd finished and put the necklace aside he laid his lips in the same place, making her shiver pleasurably.

'Are you sure?' he said softly.

Through the pounding of her blood she managed to say, 'Yes,' but he was already drawing down the zip at the back of her dress.

She turned swiftly, letting the dress fall about her ankles, opening her arms to him in welcome, eager for him in every way.

'Oh, my love,' she said. 'Come to me. At last.'

It was Crystal's mocking voice in his dreams that awoke him.

'You need a rich wife, and there aren't many who are richer than her.'

He'd rejected the words, but they'd lingered, just out of sight, and now they pounced on him, shocking him into wakefulness.

He turned his head slowly to where Joanna lay still

asleep in the dawn light. Through the sheet covering her he could see the outline of her beautiful nakedness, offered to him last night with such tenderness one moment, and such fierce intensity the next. But lovelier still was the sight of her face, soft and vulnerable on the pillow.

A rich wife!

It was horrible but true. Last night, overcome by both his love and his desire, he'd managed to believe that the disparity between them was unimportant. But in the cold light of day he knew it mattered.

What could he say to her? Speak of love while concealing the financial truth? His soul revolted at the thought.

Or how about, 'Marry me, and by the way I need some cash.' She knew of his debts, but not the sudden crisis of Crystal's demands. The truth would merely convince her that the past was repeating itself, and anything was better than that.

Throughout that long, passionate night he'd been awed by what he discovered in her. The warmth and generosity that were part of her everyday life also infused her lovemaking. Her gifts were bountiful, and in response his whole being, not just his body but also his spirit, had been given a release that thrilled him.

He'd been startled by the strength of his own feelings, so much more intense than his mild affection for her twelve years ago, and so much deeper than his infatuation for Crystal. But the bitter fact was that there was no honest way he could approach her.

He'd discovered the truth only when it was too late.

He slipped out of bed and put on his clothes, moving quietly. When he'd finished he came over and dropped to his knees beside the bed, his face close to hers. She lay just as before, her expression as gentle and trusting as a child's. The kiss he placed on her forehead was so light that it didn't awaken her.

'I'm sorry,' he whispered. 'Try to forgive me.'

Joanna kept her eyes closed until the last minute, knowing that when she opened them the night would be over. What came next would be as sweet, or even sweeter, but nothing would ever quite equal that first revelation.

She had never stopped loving Gustavo for one moment. All this time she'd been deluding herself.

But now there needed to be no more delusions. She could love him freely, as he loved her. She didn't doubt his love, not after last night. And she knew that, when she finally allowed herself to wake, she would see that love in his eyes, watching over her.

To prolong the moment she stretched out, letting her hand wander over the place where he should have been. Finding nothing there, she lay still a moment, then opened her eyes and sat up, surveying the room.

Apart from herself it was empty.

Something in her refused to believe what she could see, because it simply wasn't possible that after the night they had spent together he should walk out and leave her to wake alone.

She thought of that night, the passionate giving and taking, the fevered, incoherent words, the hot silences. He was a generous lover, inciting her gently, lovingly. His passion had inspired her own, taking her to heights she'd never known before.

The descent had been melancholy, but it would have been forgotten in the joy of waking in his arms.

Of course, he'd left early to avoid being seen. But why hadn't he known that she would want him to wake her first?

Stop being childish, she reproved herself. It'll be all right when you see him.

Slipping out of bed, she pulled on a robe and went to the window, looking out over the rear lawns stretching away, and there, in the distance, Gustavo's tall figure wandering under the trees.

It seemed as though he had put as much distance between them as possible.

She turned away, unable to see him through the sudden blurring in her eyes.

Downstairs she found everyone cheerful. Freddy was planning to spend the day at the dig, which was going well.

Gustavo looked up when Joanna came into the breakfast room, and gave her a brief smile, with a shadow of constraint. Frowning, she made her way over to him by the window.

'I had to leave early,' he said quietly. 'I didn't want to be found walking the corridor in the early hours.'

'Like you found me, at Rannley Towers?' she said, with an attempt at teasing. 'Only you got the wrong idea.'

'Yes, I did, didn't I?' he said with another attempt at a smile. 'I'm sorry about that.'

'Gustavo—'

'At least it can't happen again. You wouldn't like that.'

'No, but—'

He looked at her, and for a moment she saw something in his face that conflicted with his words. But then he was in command of himself again.

'Is everything all right with you?' he asked.

'No, it isn't,' she said indignantly. 'I thought we'd have more to say than this.'

'Yes, we must talk, but not here and now. Later there are things I must say to you.'

Her temper flared. 'Perhaps you need not bother. I'm beginning to think it's all been said.'

'Joanna—'

She heard the plea in his voice but was too angry to heed it.

'All right, gang,' she said brightly, approaching them. 'Let's get to work. Billy, what are you doing?'

'Renata and me are going riding with Luca,' he said, and she nodded, satisfied. Luca was the head groom, and reliable.

After that she gave all her attention to her work. Hal had discovered a hollow sound in one of the foundation walls, suggesting a hidden chamber behind it. Everyone was excited. By concentrating hard she was able to push thoughts of Gustavo aside, until Hal said, 'Look who's here.'

Gustavo was standing just outside the tent and he glanced aside, indicating for her to come out and join him. As she stepped into the sun he began to walk away.

'I have to talk to you,' he said. 'I've been doing a lot of thinking and there are things—I wasn't sure whether to tell you this, how you'd react—'

A deep apprehension was growing in her. 'Is this something you ought to have told me before last night?' she asked calmly.

'Yes,' he said after a moment. 'I think perhaps I should have done that.'

'Well, better late than never,' she said, smiling to cover her feelings.

'I'm so afraid that you'll misunderstand, and think I behaved badly.'

'Did you?'

'In a manner of speaking,' he sighed. 'I should have thought before—when I saw Crystal last night—'

He stopped because a distant sound was rapidly growing nearer.

'What's that?'

'It sounds like someone galloping hell for leather,' Joanna said, looking into the distance.

The next moment a horse came into view, ridden by Luca, the groom who had accompanied Renata and Billy that morning. Now he was alone.

Gustavo drew a sharp breath and ran towards him, followed by Joanna. As they hurried across the grass she asked, 'Why is he alone? Where are the children? Oh, God—'

'What's happened?' Gustavo called as Luca reached them.

'An accident—' he said breathlessly.

'*Billy!*' Joanna cried.

'No, no, it's the little girl. She fell. I think her shoulder is hurt. Billy is fine, but he has stayed to comfort her.'

'Where?' Gustavo rapped out.

Luca described the place and Gustavo strode off to his car, pulling out his cellphone to call an ambulance as he went. Joanna got in with him and they were on their way, with Luca in the back.

'Her head,' Gustavo snapped over his shoulder. 'Is her head injured?'

'I don't think so, *signor*,' said the wretched Luca. 'Just her shoulder.'

'Are you sure Billy isn't hurt?' Joanna urged.

'He didn't fall, I swear it,' Luca insisted.

At last the place came in sight, near a stream. There were a few trees, one of which had come down and lay on the ground. Renata, supported by Billy, was sitting up, holding her arm and sobbing.

'*Piccina…*' Gustavo dropped on his knees beside his daughter. 'It's all right. Papa's here.'

He reached out to her but then drew his hands back, afraid of hurting her.

'I'm here, *cara*,' he said again.

But his presence brought her no comfort. Instead she leaned against Billy, wailing, 'Mamma! *Mamma!*'

Gustavo got to his feet and turned away.

'I hope the ambulance won't take long,' he said in a carefully controlled voice. It gave no hint of his feelings, but she knew, without words, and placed a hand on his arm.

'Every child wants her mother at a time like this,' she said. 'Surely she'll come now?'

'You're right,' he said curtly, and began to make another call. But after a moment he hung up and said in frustration, 'Her phone is switched off.'

'What about her home telephone?'

'I don't know her number now she's moved back to Rome. I'll have to call her lawyer— Thank God! There's the ambulance.'

'Can't we come to the hospital with you?'

'Thank you, but no.'

She understood. He wanted to be alone with Renata, and seize the chance to grow closer to her.

She felt stunned by the suddenness of events. There was nothing for her to do but watch as the ambulance arrived and departed a few minutes later.

'Are you sure you're all right?' she said to Billy.

'I'm fine, Mum.'

'I'll drive you back to the dig,' Luca said.

She'd thought that Gustavo might call her with news, but hours passed with no word from him. Then, in the late afternoon, a taxi drew up, and Gustavo and Renata got out. He carried her up the steps in his arms, and Joanna saw that she seemed to be asleep.

'Just a broken arm,' he told Joanna and Laura. 'They didn't even want to keep her in overnight. They gave her a light anaesthetic and she's still a bit dopey, so she needs to go straight to bed.'

'I'll take her,' Laura said, reaching out.

'No, I'll carry her up,' he said.

Joanna went up the stairs ahead of him, reaching Renata's room first, opening the door and waiting as he walked slowly along the corridor. She had a glimpse of his face as he looked down at his child, and saw there everything he dreaded the world knowing, his shattering love for his child and his heartbreak at her rejection.

'I'll help you undress her,' she told Laura as Gustavo laid Renata on the bed.

'I'll wait outside,' he said.

Renata remained drowsy until almost the last minute, but then she awoke suddenly and began to cry.

'Mamma,' she wept. 'Mamma, Mamma.'

Joanna opened the door. 'Did you manage to contact Crystal?'

'No. I got her new address from the lawyer but when I call I get the answerphone.'

He went to the bed and tried to take his daughter in his arms, but she pushed him away with her one good arm, then buried her face in the pillow and sobbed.

'Renata, *carissima*,' he begged, stroking her hair. 'Please—'

'I want Mamma.'

Suddenly a thought came to Joanna, so startling that she moved away to the window, where Gustavo couldn't see her face.

This might be the thing that would bring Crystal back,

perhaps permanently. Was that what Gustavo secretly wanted, both to save himself from ruin and for the little girl's sake?

She tried to resist the idea, but she knew it would explain his uneasiness about last night. And what else could explain it?

But it wouldn't happen, she assured herself, because Crystal would never willingly return.

She went back to the bed where Gustavo was still sitting, his head bent in anguish at his inability to comfort his daughter. Renata's cries had gone beyond words. The noise that came from her now was a soft wail of endless despair.

Joanna took a deep breath. There was no decision to make. It had already been made by forces beyond her control.

'Gustavo,' she said, 'you've got to get Crystal. I don't care what it takes but get her here.'

He met her eyes for just a moment. 'You're right,' he said briefly.

For a moment she thought he would kiss Renata, but he stopped himself, looking at her sadly. Then he left.

Joanna stood at the window and watched him drive away, wondering what she had done, and how it would turn out. But there'd been no alternative. She knew that.

CHAPTER ELEVEN

OVER supper Billy told her and Freddy everything.

'There was this fallen tree, Mum, and she said she could jump it. Luca told her not to but she wouldn't listen.'

'Women don't,' Freddy said wisely, and they exchanged nods, man to man.

'Anyway, she jumped and fell off as the horse landed. It was really scary. I thought she'd broken her neck.'

'No, just her arm,' Joanna said. 'But you're a hero, staying with her like that.'

'She kept talking about her mum, saying she'd come and take her away now. Then she'd cry even more.'

'I expect that arm hurts a lot,' Freddy observed.

'No, it's more than that,' Billy insisted. 'Even before this, she talks about her mother wanting her, and then she cries. I think she knows it's not true. She won't admit it, but part of her is beginning to suspect.'

'Well, her mother's coming now,' Joanna said. 'It may all work out for them. Isn't it your bedtime?'

Billy assumed a mulish look, but Freddy clapped him on the back and said, 'Come on. Let's finish that talk we were having.'

They went off together.

It was late at night before Gustavo returned. At first Joanna thought he was alone, but then he opened the rear door and Crystal climbed out. Even from this distance Joanna could see that she was in a thunderous sulk. She saw Gustavo point towards the house, then take her arm firmly to draw her inside.

Joanna opened the door to see them approaching and stood back while Crystal approached the child, who, by now, had fallen asleep. She sat on the bed and gave her a little shake. Renata's eyes opened. She gave a glad cry at the sight of her mother's face, and the next moment they were locked in each other's arms.

Joanna could just make out the words Crystal was murmuring, words of motherly love and reassurance. She gave Gustavo a puzzled look, and he drew her out into the corridor.

'She does it beautifully, doesn't she?' he said. 'You wouldn't think I practically had to frogmarch her into the car. Now she'll play the role of the loving mother until it bores her, then she'll go again, leaving me to pick up the pieces.'

'What's happening to her other child?'

'Safe in the apartment with Elena, his nanny.'

'So Crystal tried not to come?'

'Yes, but I persuaded her,' he said, his eyes glinting. 'I also persuaded her to bring some clothes because she's going to stay a few days, whether she likes it or not.'

His face was hard, forbidding. Joanna would have given a lot to know his thoughts, but she suddenly realised that in this family quarrel she was an outsider.

'I have things to get on with,' she said heavily. 'I hope this all works out as you want.'

For a few days she kept well clear of the family, eating at the dig and working late into the evening, determinedly keeping her thoughts on her work. She refused to speculate on what might be happening between Gustavo and Crystal. That way lay madness.

She came inside late one night to hear music coming

from the radio. Through an open door she could just make out Crystal swaying in the dance. So she and Gustavo had reached that stage, she thought.

But it was Freddy, not Gustavo, who was dancing with Crystal. They moved in perfect time together and looked good, Joanna had to admit. Gustavo was sitting at a table, writing. He looked up and saw Joanna standing in the doorway.

'Come in and join us,' he said, with a touch of relief in his voice. 'I'll have something sent in.'

He rang the bell and a cold supper appeared so quickly that it was clear it had been already waiting.

'I'll just run upstairs…' she said, eyeing the food with pleasure.

'No need,' Freddy said, emerging from the dance. 'Billy's fast asleep. We swam for miles.'

'Oh, yes,' she said, remembering. 'There's a swimming pool in the grounds, isn't there?'

'I've had it cleaned out,' Gustavo said, bringing her a glass of wine. 'You're all welcome to use it. A day off in the pool would probably do your team good.'

'Thank you. Yes, I think we'd like that.'

She sipped her wine before asking, 'How is Renata?'

'Doing well,' Gustavo said quietly.

'She's so much better,' Crystal said sweetly. 'I took her to the pool and she paddled in the shallow end. The poor little soul wanted to go in with Freddy and Billy, but she can't, because of her arm.'

'But I'm sure she was happy sitting on the side with you,' Joanna said. 'It means so much to her to have you here.'

'But of course,' Crystal said prettily. 'Nobody can replace a mother, can they?'

More music came from the radio and she began twirling around the room again, looking gloriously pretty and several years younger than her real age. Freddy joined her and they bounded around like teenagers.

Joanna finished her supper, bid them goodnight and went to the library, where most of the others were still up. They looked tired and disgruntled.

'I thought we'd be through the wall into that chamber by now,' Lily grumbled.

'The wall's twice as thick as the others,' Claire said.

'I know.' Joanna flexed her hands, which were still painful from the day's work. 'But we'll be through soon, won't we, Hal? Hal?'

'He's been asleep in that chair for the last hour,' Danny said. 'And we're all knackered.'

'Fine, then let's have some time off. There's a swimming pool here and we're all invited to spend the day in it.'

Everyone cheered, even Hal, who seemed to cheer in his sleep.

'Tomorrow, then,' Joanna said.

They gathered at the pool next day, all giving yells of delight as the clear blue water came into sight, glinting under the sun. In minutes they were all jumping in.

Joanna tried not to look as Gustavo appeared with Crystal and Renata, both in bathing suits. They seemed like a family, which, in a sense, they were. Just as she, Freddy and Billy were.

Billy was already in the deep end, crowing as he climbed onto Freddy's shoulders and dived. But he swam the length of the pool when he saw Renata arrive and sit at the top of the steps that led down into the shallow end. Joanna stayed where she was, in earshot.

Crystal and Renata had their heads together, and

Joanna heard the word 'Toni' several times, and saw Renata smile at the mention of her baby half-brother.

'Look,' Crystal said, reaching into her bag and taking out a photo album. 'Joanna, you haven't seen my baby, have you?'

He was a beautiful child, full of smiles. Picture after picture showed him beaming with delight, mostly enfolded in his mother's arms, while she looked down on him with an expression of delight.

'I keep these with me always,' she told Joanna.

'Hey, Crystal!' That was Freddy's voice, calling from the pool. Crystal gave a shriek and danced into the water.

As soon as she was gone Renata dived into her bag, rummaging through with hands that grew increasingly frantic, until at last she gave up and pushed the bag aside.

'What's the matter?' Gustavo came close to ask her.

'She's just discovered that Crystal doesn't keep any pictures of her, the way she does of Toni,' Joanna muttered. 'Damn her!'

Gustavo swore under his breath and went to sit beside Renata. For once she didn't turn away from him, and Joanna guessed that Crystal's presence now made him one of the 'good guys'. She even gave him a smile, although it was clearly an effort, and Joanna guessed that Billy's presence helped.

She swam down the pool to find Freddy, and join him in a sandwich from the buffet Gustavo had arranged at the side of the pool.

'This is the life,' he said, stretched out luxuriously on the grass while she filled his glass with wine. 'How can I arrange to live like this all the time?'

'What you need is another rich wife,' she observed, without resentment.

'Ah, now, that's not fair,' he protested. 'I was nuts about you. You know that.'

'Yes, you were,' she agreed. 'But just how nuts would you have been if I hadn't had a nice fat bank balance?'

He considered this seriously. 'The point is that you were always likely to. I had just enough cash of my own to move among moneyed people, so I met rich ladies. The odds were always in my favour.'

She had to laugh at this. His good-natured face was so guileless.

'I'm surprised you're not playing the odds again by this time,' she said.

He frowned. 'The problem is, knowing exactly what the odds are.'

'How do you mean?'

'If I did marry again, I suppose the allowance you pay me would stop.'

'You mean I might regard it as her job to support you, rather than mine?'

'I can imagine a lot of women being difficult about it.'

'Not me. How could you think I'd let the father of my son go short?'

He crowed with laughter. 'That's the spirit.'

'Why is it so important, anyway? If she's rich enough to afford you—'

'Yes, but a fellow likes to have a little independence,' he said, totally straight-faced, which left her speechless.

'You are totally shameless,' she said at last. 'I mean, I've never known anyone like you.'

'There isn't anyone like me. I'm the one and only. Buy while stocks last. Only I'll soon be getting a bit beyond my sell-by date, so it's time to think about the future.'

'Do you have an ideal in mind—money apart, that is?'

'Well, she shouldn't be too serious. I like to have a

good time and to blazes with tomorrow. But most women don't seem to be made like that.'

'Crystal is,' Joanna sighed.

'Yes, but she's a bit short of the readies at the moment. Gustavo still has to hand over the other half of her money, and she's asking for it faster than he can manage.'

She looked at him quickly. 'How do you know that?'

'She told me. We've got to know each other quite well in these last few days. She finds me a handy shoulder to cry on. They're having a bit of an argument about it. Hasn't he told you?'

'No, he hasn't.'

'Ah, well, he might find it a bit difficult. Reasons of delicacy and all that.' He said this as though speaking a foreign language.

After a moment he went on, 'It's a pity, because in an ideal world you and Gustavo would get married fast, and that would solve everyone's problems.'

'Freddy, are you going to be vulgar again?'

'Probably. The most practical solutions usually are vulgar to people of refined sensibilities.'

'How would you know? You wouldn't recognise a refined sensibility if it came up and bopped you on the nose.'

'Yes, I would, and I'd bop it first. Serve it right for causing so much trouble in the world.'

'What are you burbling about now?' she asked, trying to speak severely but unable not to laugh.

'I'm saying that if you were to marry Gustavo, he could afford to repay Crystal her money, and then she'd be out of his hair, and yours. And of course, once she's regained her fortune—well—'

'Are you daring to suggest—?'

'Well, you said it yourself, I need a rich wife. And I think she and I might deal very well together.'

It dawned on her that he was perfectly right. He and Crystal were ideally suited.

'And the kids would love it,' Freddy added. 'Keep it all in the family, so to speak.'

He was right about that too. In fact, he was so right in every cynical suggestion that she dived hastily back into the pool.

It was a good day and everyone felt better when they were making their way back to the house in the late afternoon, ready to dress up for a good dinner.

Joanna was down first, finding Crystal in the library.

'Are you cross with me?' Crystal asked. 'You've been giving me glowering looks all day. I hate it when people are cross with me.'

'If I'm cross it's because of the way you hurt Renata.'

'Me? I've been delightful to her.'

'How about flaunting those pictures of Toni, when you don't keep any of her?'

'Did she look in my bag? She shouldn't have done.'

'She was looking for reassurance that you carry her pictures too. And you don't. That hurt her, Crystal.'

'Oh, hell!' Crystal gave a despairing sigh and ran her hands through her hair. 'Look, I— You think I'm a monster, don't you?'

'Well—I can't imagine taking as little interest in Billy as you seem to take in Renata.'

'I know, I know, but I can't help it. It's not my fault. Something happened when she was born—or rather, something didn't happen. The first time I held her I waited for that rush of love you're supposed to get, and there was absolutely nothing. I tried and tried, but I couldn't feel anything.'

Joanna remembered her first sight of Billy, and the love that had swept through her like a hurricane. She felt a moment's sympathy for Crystal, who hadn't known that incredible joy. Perhaps she shouldn't be blamed too much for being unable to bond.

But the next moment some of her sympathy evaporated, when Crystal said, 'If only she'd been a boy! I wanted a boy so much. All those months of getting thicker and uglier, and feeling awful. Of course Gustavo wanted an heir, and I wanted to give him one and get it out of the way.

'I had a bad birth. It just went on for ages and ages, and all the time I was thinking, Please let it be a boy, so I need never do this again. And then she turned out to be a girl and I was so angry.'

'Angry?'

'I was tired,' Crystal said defensively. 'I ached all over, and Gustavo was saying things like, "Never mind, darling. Next time." Like that was supposed to make me feel better. And I knew every last person on the estate was going to be disappointed in me, and I just felt fed up.'

'Fed up,' Joanna echoed. Crystal's petulant self-centredness was so overwhelming that it was almost impressive.

'Of course the estate people were interested,' she pointed out. 'If the prince doesn't have an heir it affects them all.'

'Yes, well, it was no fun being a princess,' Crystal said sulkily. 'I thought it would be, but it wasn't.'

'Is that why you married him? For the title? You didn't love him at all?'

'I don't really know,' Crystal said, considering this. 'Yes, I suppose I was in love with him, in a sort of way.

He seemed glamorous and exciting then. I thought that was how we'd live, going to all the thrilling places in the world, meeting everyone who mattered. But all Gustavo wanted was to bury himself in this place and spend every penny on it.

'Oh, we went travelling sometimes. He took me to New York every year. But even then he spent half his time on the phone to Renata's nurse, wanting to know if everything was all right. And he couldn't wait to get home. Lord, but he's dull to live with!'

'Dull? Gustavo?'

'He doesn't know how to have fun.'

'I suppose he has his own idea of fun.'

'Yes, old bones and bricks. History. Estate accounts. No, thank you!'

Suddenly she burst out, 'I can't help the way I'm made. It's not my fault. I can't make myself feel what I don't feel.'

'No, I suppose not,' Joanna sighed.

'I tried for years, but I couldn't manage it. I should never have married him. He should have married you. You're as dull as him.'

'Yes, I suppose I am,' Joanna said, without resentment.

You couldn't be angry with Crystal, she reflected. Part of her was still a child, and knew no better.

'I expect supper will be ready,' she said. 'Shall we go in?'

'Just give me a moment. I haven't called Elena yet.'

Crystal called Toni's nanny several times a day to ask about him. In a moment she was on the phone to her, and Joanna could see at once that something was wrong.

'I can hear him screaming,' she said into the phone. 'What's wrong with him? Is he ill? What do you mean, hungry? He's ill. I know he's ill.'

Gustavo came into the room, with Renata. 'What's the matter?'

'Toni's ill,' Crystal wailed. 'I must go to him at once. He might be dying.'

Gustavo took the phone from her. 'Elena? What's happened? I see. Just his feed being a few minutes late?'

'I've got to go to him,' Crystal wept.

Out of the corner of her eye Joanna saw Renata leave the room. Quietly she followed her out into the hall, up the stairs and as far as her room.

'What are you doing?' she asked as Renata began taking clothes out of drawers, hampered by only having one good arm.

'I'm going with Mamma. She wants me.'

'But—'

'She wants me,' Renata said, too decidedly to be convincing. 'If Toni's ill she won't come back, so I have to go with her.'

Gustavo appeared in the doorway and she could see from his face that he had heard. He looked quickly at Joanna, and she saw a plea for help in his eyes.

'*Carissima,*' he said.

The child turned on him. 'You can't stop me.'

'Gustavo!' That was Crystal's voice calling from the corridor. 'I'm ready to go. I have to get to Toni quickly.'

'I'm coming, Mamma,' Renata called.

'What?' Crystal came into the room, frowning. 'What did you say?'

'I'm ready to go.'

'But, darling, what are you talking about? I can't take you with me.'

'But you said—'

'I said one day—maybe—but now Toni's ill—'

'But that means you'll need me.' Renata's voice had risen to a wail.

'But—but—I'm sorry, but you've got to understand— I simply can't—'

'Renata—' Gustavo began.

'No,' Joanna said swiftly, putting her hand on his arm. 'Don't say it. This isn't a time for authority. It's a time for pleading.'

'What do you mean?'

'Don't order her,' she said softly. 'But tell her how much you need her. Plead, beg if you have to.'

'But you can see how she is—'

'Don't give Crystal the chance to reject her again. She couldn't bear it. It's your best chance. *Do it!*'

Renata was regarding her mother with eyes that held a terrible look. Gustavo got between them, dropping down to one knee and putting his hands on her shoulders.

'Carissima,' he said, 'if you want to go, I won't stop you, but please don't. Think of me if you went away. What would I do without you?'

She stood silent, uncertainty written all over her face.

'I know you'd rather go with Mamma,' Gustavo said, 'but I love you too, more than you know. Won't you stay with me? Please.'

Renata took a long breath and suddenly it was as though a great burden had fallen from her. She straightened herself, looking suddenly taller.

'I can't go with you after all, Mamma,' she said with childish dignity. 'Papa needs me to stay and look after him.'

'Thank you, my darling,' he said.

Crystal's gift for playing a part came to her rescue.

'I'm sure you're right,' she said. 'You should stay and be kind to Papa. Yes, that's what you should do.'

She repeated this, evidently feeling that it was a mantra that she should cling to.

'Now I need someone to drive me into Rome,' she said.

'The chauffeur will take you,' Gustavo said. 'I prefer to stay with my daughter.'

'If you think a chauffeur's good enough for me when I'm in such a state about my baby,' Crystal sniffed.

'Of course a chauffeur isn't good enough,' said Freddy from behind her. He'd slid into the room, unnoticed. 'I'd be glad to drive you.'

'Oh, Freddy, you're so kind and understanding,' Crystal said.

'It's my pleasure,' he said, meaning it.

Joanna followed them out and downstairs to where the car had been brought around to the front. Before getting in Freddy gave her a wink. She shook her head in disapproval, which just made him wink again.

Before returning upstairs Joanna called Crystal's Rome apartment. She knew the number after seeing Crystal dial it so often.

'Elena? She's on her way.'

The nanny gave an exasperated sigh. 'There's no need. I've fed him and he's fast asleep. There's nothing wrong with him.'

'Well, she's still on her way,' Joanna said wryly.

She joined the others for supper and didn't see Gustavo again until the end of the evening. Then he came seeking her, seizing her hands in his and holding them tight.

'Thank you with all my heart,' he said. 'I would never have thought of that. However did I manage before you came along? You've transformed everything. If only I…'

For some reason he seemed unable to go on.

'If only what?'

'If only I'd listened to your advice before,' he said, in an awkward way that told her it wasn't what he'd been going to say.

'It saved Renata's face, poor little soul,' she said sympathetically. 'This way, she's the one who made the decision.'

'And that matters?'

'Oh, yes,' she said, her mind going back twelve years. 'You've no idea how much it matters.'

He released her hands. 'I'll be grateful to you all my life,' he said. 'I only wish I knew the way to tell you what you've done for me—how much it means.'

She waited, hoping for something more, but it didn't come. He'd retreated into himself again, and whatever he might have said would remain unspoken.

CHAPTER TWELVE

FOR those working on the dig, only one thing now mattered. How soon could they work their way through the bricks concealing the secret chamber? Brick after brick was eased out, dusted off carefully, and handed up to Lily, who inspected it minutely before passing it on to Danny, who X-rayed it. Sonya then put it through a battery of other tests, including scan and radar.

Joanna's conviction grew. This was the earlier part of the old lost *palazzo*, which meant it was at least fifth century, and perhaps earlier. When the brick that should have been in the last layer was removed, revealing just one more 'last layer', Joanna led the cries of agonised exasperation.

'I can't bear any more,' Hal moaned.

'Oh, shut up, you cry-baby!' she told him, calming down and managing to laugh. 'Let's get on with it.'

It took another half-day to work through the last brick into the gap.

'We're through,' she said. 'Let's have the flashlight.'

In another moment she was shining the light through into the darkness. What she saw made her sit down suddenly, breathing hard.

'What is it?' Lily and Danny demanded in one voice.

'Take this,' she said, holding out the flashlight, 'and tell me what you see in there.'

One by one they looked, but nobody spoke a word. They were all too dumbfounded.

'I think,' Joanna said slowly, 'that I should fetch Gustavo.'

The light was fading as she reached the house and went straight to the library, where she found Gustavo at his desk with Renata, poring over an atlas, heads together.

'There's something I think you should come and see,' she said as calmly as she could manage.

She was pleased to see that he instinctively glanced at his daughter, including her in the expedition.

'I thought you'd all be coming in to supper about now,' he said.

'This is much better than supper,' she said.

A mysterious, suppressed glee in her manner made him look at her, puzzled.

'What is it?' he asked.

'Come and see,' she told him.

Renata took her father's hand. 'Let's go, Papa.'

'Yes,' he said. 'You lead the way.'

They went back in Joanna's car and found the excavation full of brilliant lights that had been hauled out from the trucks.

'We've got out another brick,' Hal confided in a tone of excitement.

'What have you discovered?' Gustavo wanted to know.

'Take this,' she said, giving him the flashlight, 'and look through there.'

He crouched down to follow the beam and she heard him draw in his breath.

'Is that—what I think it is?' he asked.

'It's gold,' Joanna said. 'I'm almost sure of it.'

'The lost treasure of Montegiano,' he murmured.

'It'll take us some days to get right in there and remove

what we find,' Joanna said cautiously. 'But it's looking good.'

'Thank you for bringing me to see it,' he said. 'If only—'

'Yes,' Joanna said, nodding in understanding. 'If only—'

'We'll have to be patient, Papa,' Renata said, speaking like a nanny. Protecting her father was something she now took very seriously.

Joanna awoke suddenly, instantly alert. It was still dark but instinct told her that there was somebody in her room.

'Who's there?' she demanded.

'It's only me,' came Gustavo's voice. 'Forgive me for coming in like this but I couldn't knock in case anyone heard. No, don't put the light on.'

She pulled herself up in bed. He was sitting on the bed and in the near-darkness she could just make out the glint in his eyes and the excitement that radiated from him.

Her pulses were racing, making it hard for her to speak. Why had he come to her room like this in the darkness?

'Gustavo, why have you come here?' she managed to whisper at last.

'I couldn't sleep. I've been lying awake thinking about everything—we're on the brink of so many things; don't you feel that?'

'Yes,' she said.

If only he would kiss her. Since their night together a shadow had seemed to fall between them, but now he was here, seeking her out as though that shadow had never been. But why didn't he touch her?

'I can't stand the waiting any longer,' he said. 'Let's do it now.'

'Let's—?'

'Go out to the dig and find out what's there.'

'Go to the dig?' she echoed in a daze.

'I know it's still dark but the dawn will break soon. There'll be enough light to find something, surely?'

She stared at his face that had grown a little clearer as the light increased.

'Is this why you came creeping into my room?' she asked, incensed.

'I know I shouldn't have done it like this, but you understand, don't you?'

'I'm beginning to.'

He didn't seem to notice a slightly grim edge to her voice. He was possessed by his own excitement over whatever might be found. Clearly this was the only thing he could focus on.

'I'll join you downstairs in a minute,' she said.

He had the car's engine already running when she got in, and in ten minutes they were there. She got out some lighting and they descended into the foundations.

'We managed to get another couple of bricks out,' she said. 'You can see better now.'

She flooded the chamber with light, while he gazed through, drawing in a slow breath.

'It's almost close enough to touch,' he said, trying to reach in. 'No, I can't get through that hole.'

'Here, take the light. I'm thinner.'

She reached forward, easing herself through the hole until she could just touch something. It came off in her hand and she had to grab it.

'Pull me back,' she said quickly.

He hauled her towards him so fast that she had to hook her arm about his neck to steady herself. He held on, not letting her go, but breathing fast.

'I'm not sure that I dare to look at it,' he said. 'It matters too much.'

'Does it?' she said, and she couldn't keep a certain sadness out of her voice. This wasn't what she had hoped mattered to him.

'More than anything you could know,' he said fervently.

'In that case,' she said calmly, 'let's look at it.'

He lowered her to the ground and they sat down on a low wall while she held up the object she had found.

It was a large brooch, made of some yellowish metal, with stones embedded in it that looked like bits of cheap old coloured glass.

'Oh,' he said in a deflated voice.

'What do you mean, "oh"?' she asked through her rising excitement.

'Cheap and nasty,' he said heavily. 'Why did they bother to preserve it?'

'Cheap and nasty?' she asked indignantly. 'Do you think jewels looked the same fifteen hundred years ago as they do now? They didn't shine and glitter like modern stones.'

'Yes, but these…' He stopped as her excitement began to get through to him. 'Do you mean that those bits of glass are—?'

'The last time I found something with "bits of glass" it sold for five million dollars,' she said. 'I'm sticking my neck out, but I think it's real—real gold, real rubies, real emeralds—'

She got no further. His arms were about her, hugging her so tightly that she was breathless. The brooch fell, unnoticed, to the ground as he kissed her again and again.

'Gustavo,' she said, laughing and kissing him back.

'We won,' he cried exultantly. 'We won. It's all right; everything's wonderful.'

'Is it?' she asked, her head reeling. 'Well, I know you're going to be very rich—'

'But that's what's wonderful, don't you see? I can ask you to marry me now.'

She placed her hands on his shoulders, frowning a little.

'Now? You can only ask now?'

'Of course. I'm independent now. I won't look like a fortune-hunter to you *now*.'

Her frown deepened. 'You never did look like a fortune-hunter to me. Put me down.'

He did so, while still keeping hold of her.

'If you only knew how hopeless it looked to me—how could I approach you when I needed your money so badly?'

'Why shouldn't you? You did it once before. I didn't blame you then. Why should you think I'd blame you now?'

'But can't you see that this is different? When we met the first time—it was a bargain on both sides. We knew the terms before we even met. In its way it was an honest transaction. But now—'

'But now we've made love,' she said slowly. 'And that makes a difference. You'll be saying next that I compromised your honour.' She gave a mirthless laugh.

'If anyone compromised it, I did. I tried to tell you that there were things I should have said first—'

'But I already knew you were short of money. You needed to raise cash to repay Crystal. I think you told me that the first day. What were you doing? Warning me off?'

'Of course not. You were just an old friend I felt I

could trust. It was only later that it mattered so much—after London… *Hell!*'

He ran his hands through his hair. He wasn't good at this. He preferred things to be straightforward.

'After London—' he tried again '—I thought we were closer—'

'So did I—'

'If Freddy hadn't appeared—well, he did, and I had to be patient. I knew our time would come—it had to.'

'The night of the party, the night Crystal appeared.'

'Yes, she put all sorts of ugly ideas into my head.'

'Trust her to do that! You shouldn't have listened.'

'She wants the rest of her money at once. Try not listening to that.'

'I know. Freddy told me. The two of them are rapidly becoming as thick as thieves, but so what? How can they affect us?'

'She suggested that I marry you to repay her. Did Freddy tell you that?'

'No, but he thought of it for himself.'

'I'll bet he did. I'll bet he's slavering at the prospect.'

'What does he matter?' she cried. 'Why must you tie yourself in knots about this?'

'Because that night I made love to you,' he said frantically, 'I did it because I wanted to. I wanted you more than I've ever wanted anything or anyone, but how can you ever believe that?'

'Because you've just told me.'

'Well, I would, wouldn't I? If I'm after your money that's just what I'd do. Perhaps you should think before believing a word I say.'

'Why are you so determined to put the case for the prosecution?' she cried.

'Because nobody else is going to put it.'

'Gustavo, I heard the case for the prosecution years ago. I've lived with it. Now I want to hear the other one.'

'You should be cautious—I had a motive for behaving badly.'

'Some people thought you were behaving badly when you married Crystal,' she flung at him. 'But you didn't care. You outfaced them because that was how much you loved her. So why can't you outface people for me?'

'Darling—'

'Don't call me darling, you hypocrite.'

'I love you, and I'll damned well call you what I like. Or doesn't it mean anything that I love you?'

There! He'd said it!

After all these years he'd said that he loved her, and instead of being the sweet, glorious moment she'd dreamed of, it had come as part of a stupid quarrel.

But it wasn't stupid. It struck at the heart of her love and what that love meant to her.

'It would have meant something if you did love me,' she said slowly. 'But actually I come some way down your list of priorities.'

'I don't know what you're talking about,' he said distractedly. 'I know this isn't the way it's supposed to happen—'

'To hell with what's supposed to happen!' she cried. 'You've spent so much of your life doing what you were *supposed* to do that you've forgotten how to do anything else. Why can't you just follow your heart, like you did with her?'

'I wish you'd leave her out of it.'

'How can I? You loved her so much that you didn't care what anyone thought, or even what you thought of yourself. Now it's different. Your priorities are first, your pride; second, your reputation; third, me.'

'That's unfair.'

'The truth is often unfair, and it is the truth. Well, it's not good enough. I don't want a half-love. I want one that matters so much that you'll trample everything else down for me, like you did before. And I can't have it, not from you, anyway. I even got better from Freddy.'

'Freddy was a fortune-hunter.'

She sighed. 'Gustavo, if I started worrying about the motives of men who had less than me I'd die an old maid. It includes most of them. I have my own standards, and that doesn't include a man's bank balance, or lack of it. I don't care! I only care how much he loves me.'

'And I've told you that I do.'

'No, you don't. What you love is your own opinion of yourself as a decent man.'

'And you? You don't love me at all, do you?'

'How the hell do you know?'

'Because you're finding excuses to back off, just like last time. Isn't that true?'

She was about to tell him everything, but her temper had risen and hell would freeze over before she made a declaration of love here and now. Her heart was bitter with disappointment that it had come to this.

'I think we should go home now,' she said. 'This isn't the time or place.'

'I think it is.'

'Don't try to talk to me, Gustavo. I'm so angry I may never want to talk to you again.'

'I don't understand you.'

'No, you don't, do you? That's one thing we can agree on. You've never understood anything about me. Not then, not now.'

She stormed off, climbed out of the dig in a rage, ran to the car and drove away.

She got halfway back to the house before common sense returned and she remembered that he had no means of transport. Groaning, she turned back and drove until she saw him.

'Get in,' she said through gritted teeth. 'And don't say a word to me, ever again, do you understand?'

'No,' he said in a hollow voice. 'I don't understand anything.'

'Then just keep quiet anyway.'

Over the next few days the full extent of the treasure was revealed, and it was greater than anyone's hopes.

Joanna's professional pride warred with her personal frustration and misery.

She could have had it all and she'd thrown it away because of some stupid, niggling bother.

No, she stopped herself there. It hadn't been stupid. And she couldn't have had it all. She could have had only the small portion Gustavo had been willing to offer. He could love her *if*…

And that 'if' damned him. If everything else was right. If he could keep his pride as well. With Crystal he'd thrown all other thoughts to the winds. With her there was an 'if'. And though it broke her heart a second time, she would not accept a conditional love in return for her wholehearted one.

There were plenty of other things to think of. It was time for Billy to go back to England and the boarding-school he attended. He liked being there, but she knew everything would have been happier if she'd settled in Italy and brought him to live here.

Freddy was taking him to England and staying a couple of days before returning to Rome and settling in a hotel near Crystal. He, at least, was over the moon about developments. So was Crystal, according to Freddy.

On the night before Freddy's departure Gustavo forced himself, like a good host, to join his unwanted guest in the library.

'May I get you another drink?' he asked politely.

'Don't mind if you do.' Freddy held out the glass and Gustavo refilled it.

'Is your packing all done?'

'Yes, don't worry, I'll be out of your hair first thing in the morning.'

'I hope you don't feel that you haven't been welcome here,' Gustavo said, forcing himself to remain courteous.

'Oh, I can make myself welcome anywhere,' Freddy said, slightly changing the meaning. 'It's been a good visit. I've seen plenty of my son, and I'm easier in my mind about you.'

'About me?' Gustavo said in surprise. 'Why should you be concerned about me?'

'I'm not. You can jump off a bridge for all I care. No offence, of course.'

'None taken,' Gustavo assured him.

'No, I'm thinking of you and Joanna. Plus, of course, you and Billy. But Billy says you're OK.'

'That's very kind of him,' Gustavo said cautiously. 'But I don't quite see—'

'Oh, for the love of heaven!' Freddy groaned. 'You and Joanna have been pussyfooting about for twelve years. Don't you think that's enough?'

'I think you've misunderstood the situation—'

'You mean you weren't engaged? Funny, everyone said you were.'

'If you were at my wedding I'm surprised you didn't get the whole story then.'

'I did, in several versions. Never quite known which one to believe.'

'Well, let's leave it that way.'

'How can we leave it?' Freddy demanded, aggrieved. 'Sooner or later you're going to marry Joanna and be Billy's stepfather—'

As always when the conversation turned to personal matters Gustavo felt himself grow tense.

'I don't know where you get such an idea—' he began.

'Everyone knows. Here, fill that up again, there's a good fellow.'

He held out his glass and Gustavo refilled it mechanically. Then he filled his own glass, drained it, refilled it.

'Then everyone is mistaken,' he said firmly. 'There's no question of it.'

Freddy gave vent to an extremely rude word, expressive of disbelief and derision.

'What's the matter with you two?' he demanded. 'You're crazy about each other, so where's the big problem? Lord, if I ever knew such a pair! Just because you made a mess of it once it doesn't mean you have to go on making a mess of it, does it?'

'Signor Manton—'

'Call me Freddy. It won't kill you, after all the other names you've been calling me under your breath. I know you don't like me. So what? I don't much like you.'

'Would you be good enough to tell me what I've done to incur your dislike?' Gustavo said, at his most wooden.

'Damned well ruined my marriage.'

'I don't know what you mean.'

'I can believe that,' Freddy said, a tad wildly. 'You're exactly the fellow who wouldn't have any idea what I was talking about. I'm talking about my wife being in love with you, that's what I'm talking about.'

'Joanna was never in love with me.'

'Don't tell me. I lived with her for eight years and I know her a sight better than you do. I was in love with that girl. D'you know, I was faithful to her for *four whole years*, including when she was pregnant.'

'You are to be commended,' Gustavo snapped with an irony that was lost on Freddy.

'That's what I think. Four years. It makes me faint to think of it, even now. Where's that decanter?'

He filled his own glass again. Gustavo was staring at him.

'Four years,' Freddy repeated, sounding more dismayed by the minute. 'And much good it did me. We never had a chance. And why? Because she was in love with you from the first.'

Gustavo found his voice at last.

'But that is not true. Joanna was delighted to end our engagement—'

'Oh, for pity's sake!' Freddy said impatiently. 'Wise up. Of course she didn't want to end it, but what did you expect her to do? Wear the willow for you, and let the world see how much she minded? Do you think she has so little self-respect?'

The air seemed to be singing in Gustavo's ears.

'She told you this?' he asked in a strange voice.

'Not in so many words, but bit by bit I've pieced it together. At your wedding nobody could talk about anything else but the groom marrying one girl when he'd been engaged to another one a week earlier.

'When I met Joanna I thought you were off your head to have let her go. My goodness, she was a cracking little dancer! How we kicked up our heels that night! It was her way of showing the world that she was fancy-free. Which she wasn't.'

'That is not what she told me,' Gustavo said slowly.

'She told you what she knew you wanted to hear. The fact is that she was madly in love with you, but she saw you kissing the other girl, so she gave you your release papers, and fed you some cock-and-bull story to make it easy for you.'

He paused to see if Gustavo would speak, but there was no sound. Gustavo's eyes seemed to burn into him.

'When we met again a year later, I thought she might be over you,' Freddy went on. 'But she wasn't. Mind you, I wasn't sure until after we were married. I may not be the sharpest tool in the box but I know when I'm making love to a woman who's pretending I'm another man.'

Like a shaft of lightning a memory came back to Gustavo.

'More than one way of being unfaithful,' he murmured. 'That's what you said.'

'That's right. Jo was always strictly faithful to me in the technical sense, but there were always three of us in the bed, if you know what I mean.'

'But…' Gustavo struggled for the right words, trying not to yield too easily to the spurt of joy that was mounting inside him '…this is only a theory. You might have misunderstood—'

'Well, I didn't. I know that because we once had a bit of a barney and she virtually admitted it. She was fond of me in her way, and it was a good marriage to start with. We can share jokes, you see, and that can paper over a lot of cracks for a while. But when it came down to it, you were always the one.

'That's partly why I turned up at Etta's wedding, because I'd heard a rumour that you and she were going to be there together, and you were divorced. I wanted to talk about Billy as well, but, as Jo pointed out, I could have done that by phone.

'I needed to see you, get the lie of the land. That's also why I barged in on you in that rude way. I wanted to catch you unawares. Yes, yes, I know I'm a vulgarian. Let's take that bit as read. Anyway, I found out what I wanted to know.'

'And what do you think you found out?'

'She's nuts about you, you're nuts about her. End of story. Or it should be if you weren't such a pair of chumps. Get on with it, for Pete's sake, before I lose patience.'

Gustavo sat in silence, feeling as though something had winded him.

'Did it really never occur to you,' Freddy asked kindly, 'that Jo did what she knew you wanted, and broke her own heart in the process?'

Gustavo shook his head.

'Damned if I see how you could have missed it.'

Gustavo gave a faint smile, directed at himself.

'Maybe I'm not the sharpest tool in the box, either,' he admitted.

'No "maybe" about it. Isn't it time you did something? Or are you going to wait another twelve years?'

Gustavo slammed his glass down.

'No,' he said. 'I'm not.'

In the hall he met Billy.

'Have you seen my dad?'

'In the library. Have you seen your mother?'

'In her room.'

'Thanks.'

'Thanks.'

He marched into Joanna's room without knocking. She

was just drying off after stepping out of the shower, and she whirled on him indignantly.

'You've got a nerve—' she said, trying to grab the towel.

'I have now. I lost my nerve for a while but I've got it back. We've got to forget all the nonsense we talked the other night because...'

It should have been so easy, he thought distractedly. Where were the speeches of love, the declarations of passion that had come so easily the other time?

But the other time hadn't mattered like this, and suddenly he was tongue-tied. The only words that would come were—

'Is your ex-husband an honest man?'

'What?'

'Is he an honest man? When he says you love me, that you've always loved me, going right back to last time—can I believe him?'

She stared at him, incredulous. He met her eyes, his own filled with a terrible intensity that showed what this meant to him. For a moment the whole world seemed to hang in the balance.

'Yes,' she said at last. 'You can believe him. I fell in love with you back then. I knew you didn't love me but I'd have married you and hoped for the best. I was going to make you love me. Only then Crystal turned up and I knew it was no use. You can't make people love you.'

'No,' he said slowly. 'You can only wait and hope that their eyes will open and they'll see the truth before it's too late.'

He grasped her shoulders so urgently that the last of the towel slipped to the floor. She didn't notice.

'Tell me it isn't too late for us,' he begged.

Her eyes shone. 'It will never be too late as far as I'm concerned.'

'Since we met again I've known that you were the one and only, but telling you so was impossible. There seemed to be so many things in the way, but they were all fantasies. I'd have known that if I were seeing straight.

'I said once that you shouldn't have released me, but if you hadn't it would never have worked out well for us. We could never have had then the marriage that we're going to have now.'

'Are we?'

He took her in his arms. 'Yes,' he said, 'we are.'

It was a kiss to mark the end of the lonely years and seal a promise.

'Tell me that you love me,' he whispered against her lips.

'I've always loved you, and I always will. Gustavo, my darling, are you quite sure?'

'I've never been more sure of anything in my life.'

'People will call you a fortune-hunter.'

'They can call me what they like as long as you call me husband. I was blind for far too long. But now I can see the way ahead, and it's there for both of us.'

He lifted her up in his arms, holding her against his chest.

'Come, my darling,' he said. 'No more waiting. Our time has come, and nothing will ever part us again.'

PREGNANT: FATHER NEEDED by Barbara McMahon

(Babies on the Way…)

Widow Amber Woodworth is making a new life for herself, as an independent, single mum-to-be. Her new neighbour, Adam Carruthers, is a sexy fireman…but Amber's determined not to get involved again, especially to a man who, like her late husband, puts his life on the line – every day…

A NANNY FOR KEEPS by Liz Fielding   *(Heart to Heart)*

Jacqui Moore is on the run – from being a nanny! She can't bear the thought of getting close to a child again, only to lose that love in a heartbeat. Until she meets little orphaned Maisie and becomes her nanny for one night. Nights turn into weeks and Jacqui's emotions are in turmoil. The master of the house, Harry Talbot, has stolen her heart…and there's nowhere left to run.

THE BRIDAL CHASE by Darcy Maguire

To help her sister, Roxanne Gray takes on a job which means she has to spend a lot of time with successful architect Cade Taylor Watson. He's gorgeous! – but strictly off-limits. Only Cade is more than keen on Roxanne – and he begins a chase which he hopes will end at the altar!

MARRIAGE LOST AND FOUND by Trish Wylie

Abbey's boyfriend has just proposed. There's just one problem: she has a husband she hasn't seen since he left her at the airport and never came back! Ethan lost his memory after an accident, so when he gets Abbey's letter, demanding a divorce, he's determined to meet the wife he didn't know he had…

On sale 1st July 2005

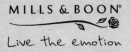

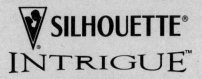

FREE!

4 Books
and a surprise gift!

We would like to take this opportunity to thank you for reading this Mills & Boon® book by offering you the chance to take FOUR more specially selected titles from the Tender Romance™ series absolutely FREE! We're also making this offer to introduce you to the benefits of the Reader Service™—

- ★ **FREE home delivery**
- ★ **FREE gifts and competitions**
- ★ **FREE monthly Newsletter**
- ★ **Exclusive Reader Service offers**
- ★ **Books available before they're in the shops**

Accepting these FREE books and gift places you under no obligation to buy, you may cancel at any time, even after receiving your free shipment. Simply complete your details below and return the entire page to the address below. You don't even need a stamp!

YES! Please send me 4 free Tender Romance books and a surprise gift. I understand that unless you hear from me, I will receive 6 superb new titles every month for just £2.75 each, postage and packing free. I am under no obligation to purchase any books and may cancel my subscription at any time. The free books and gift will be mine to keep in any case.

N5ZEF

Ms/Mrs/Miss/Mr ....Initials...............................
BLOCK CAPITALS PLEASE
Surname ....
Address..

....
....Postcode ....

Send this whole page to:
UK: FREEPOST CN81, Croydon, CR9 3WZ